Bluecoat

A BROOKE HILL NOVEL

BLUECOAT
A.E. LEE

NEW YORK
LONDON • NASHVILLE • MELBOURNE • VANCOUVER

Bluecoat

A Brooke Hill Novel

Published in New York, New York, by Morgan James Publishing. Morgan James is a trademark of Morgan James, LLC. www.MorganJamesPublishing.com

Proudly distributed by Publishers Group West®

Morgan James BOGO™

A **FREE** ebook edition is available for you or a friend with the purchase of this print book.

CLEARLY SIGN YOUR NAME ABOVE

Instructions to claim your free ebook edition:
1. Visit MorganJamesBOGO.com
2. Sign your name CLEARLY in the space above
3. Complete the form and submit a photo of this entire page
4. You or your friend can download the ebook to your preferred device

ISBN 9781636983905 paperback
ISBN 9781636983912 ebook
Library of Congress Control Number: 2023950538

Cover Design by:
Rachel Lopez
www.r2cdesign.com

Interior Design by:
Christopher Kirk
www.GFSstudio.com

Morgan James is a proud partner of Habitat for Humanity Peninsula and Greater Williamsburg. Partners in building since 2006.

Get involved today! Visit: www.morgan-james-publishing.com/giving-back

To my own fiery, red-headed best friend

PROLOGUE

Four years ago

Tears gathered in the corners of Brooke Hill's sky-blue eyes, the liquid making them look like glass. She wasted no time in brushing away the emotion with her fingertips; there would be time for private celebration and reflection later. Her long, dark-chocolate hair was pulled into a tight bun, and she stood at attention in the packed room. Brooke's promotion ceremony was underway, a milestone she had been working toward for nearly five years.

After giving the crowd a brief biography—how she was a Fairfax, Virginia native, an upstanding citizen, and a half-decade-long distinguished officer of the Fairfax County Police Department who'd just aced her promotional exam—Sergeant Jeff Willows turned to Brooke and nodded. "Raise your right hand," he said.

Brooke did as instructed. The weight of the new, dark blue jacket, with five gold buttons and the emblem of the FCPD stitched on the right shoulder sleeve, reminded her of the ten-pound weighted blanket she had used in high school to calm her anxiety. Grabbing the bottom of the jacket with her left hand, she held it straight, the cameras snapping in the background.

"Repeat after me: 'I, Brooke Elizabeth Hill'…" Willows' deep voice echoed through the space.

"I, Brooke Elizabeth Hill …" Brooke's voice, on the other hand, faltered, causing her to stand all the straighter to combat any show of nerves.

"Do solemnly swear to continue upholding the laws of the land, to protect and defend, and to serve …"

A salty-sweet, metallic taste hit Brooke's tongue. She realized she'd been biting her lip, and she quickly pressed her mouth into a straight line to stop the seeping blood. She repeated what the sergeant had spoken.

After another minute, his final words pierced her heart with joy: "Please join me in congratulating *Detective* Brooke Hill."

Applause erupted, and Brooke stared stoically at her gathered friends, family, and co-workers, as well as the three other officers receiving promotions that morning. As she turned to take her seat, she heard her younger sister, Cassie, holler her name above the commotion. A smile escaped her lips. *Always one for theatrics,* she thought.

Once she sat down, Brooke fingered the brass detective's pin on her blue coat and blew out the breath she had been holding. She'd done it! For a brief moment, she focused on her next goal—becoming the head of the Domestic Violence Unit. *Look out, Benji,* she thought, *here I come.*

She looked over at her new boss, Lieutenant Sheila Adams, a tall and lanky black woman with a contagious smile. She nodded her congratulations at Brooke. Brooke was looking forward to working for her.

After nodding back, Brooke turned her full attention on the handsome officer now standing in front of Sergeant Willows, another newly minted detective awaiting his recognition.

CHAPTER 1

Present day

"**Y**ou think you're gonna call the police? I'll kill you before you even get a chance to finish dialing!"

At six-foot-two, Don Reese towered over his petite wife, Ann, a fact he never ceased to use to his advantage. As Ann backed into the upstairs hallway from their bedroom, he followed.

She felt as if he was stalking her like some sort of injured prey. He was close enough that she could feel his hot breath on her face. "I'll chop up your body before the police ever get a chance to ring the doorbell!" he bellowed. His hands flexed at his sides, as if he couldn't wait to grab her and make his threat a reality.

Already damp from the full glass of water Don had thrown at her earlier, she braced herself as she stopped and gazed up into his face, wondering how she had fallen in love with this man. She knew this look on his face, the way his eyes went from that beautiful brown color to black with rage. Violence was imminent.

I have to get away from him. He's going to kill me!

She turned before his hands could take her prisoner and sprinted down the stairs of their new, million-dollar Craftsman, the house meant to be their dream home and where their two children would enjoy their childhood—and thrive.

When she reached the bottom of the stairs, she raised the cell phone she was gripping in her hand and dialed the first number: *nine*. Then she froze. Ann realized the fatal flaw in her plan. Her two small children were asleep in their beds … back upstairs.

Don stood at the top of the staircase and mocked her. "What are you going to do? Call the cops? You don't have the balls!"

She tapped the next number: *one*. This only angered him more. "You know what? Forget this! I'm going to light this place up! I'm going to burn this house down, and you won't have a chance to get the kids out before the whole thing goes up in flames!"

He descended the stairs and moved past her, heading toward the garage. Ann stiffened—she knew there were two full gas cans in there. The realization she had one shot to get the kids and herself to safety before it was too late hit her like a heavyweight boxer landing a final, lights out blow.

As soon as Don was out of sight, her brain found her legs, and she sprinted back up the stairs and into her daughter's room. Her heart skipped with gratitude when she found her son there too. *Thank you, God!* They were still awake, covered to their chins with the pink comforter, no doubt terrified with all of the screaming.

"Connor, Emma, we need to go. Grab your lovies. We need to leave now!" The kids did not ask questions. The urgency in their mother's voice and the look on her face said it all. Emma grabbed her white unicorn from her bedside table. Connor was already clutching his stuffed puppy in his tiny hand.

The three of them raced down the stairs, out the front door, and into the muggy night, not bothering to shut the door behind them. The heavy nocturnal air did nothing to slow the adrenaline pumping through Ann's veins.

Once they reached their neighbor's white-columned front porch across the street, Ann ushered her two crying children toward the double wooden doors and rang the bell. Then she turned toward her house. She could see clearly through the still-open front door, right into her foyer.

There, rounding the corner and entering the hallway that led to the kitchen at the back of the house was Don—a red gas can in one hand, a lighter in the other.

CHAPTER 2

"This is it!" Detective Brooke Hill's words, spoken only to the air around her, gave her a rush of adrenaline.

Just as she was about to get out of her white Camry, "Africa" by Toto came on the radio. It was *her* song, shared with her long-time best friend, Jacs. Fond memories of Jacs' mom flooded her; she'd blare the song through the car speakers anytime she drove carpool during Brooke and Jacs' childhood.

Parked in the police station lot, Brooke knew if any of her colleagues saw her jamming out to Toto—complete with some pretty fantastic air drumming, if she said so herself—razzing would ensue, and she would be mortified. It was, after all, her first day in her new, important role.

As the song ended, Brooke pulled down her driver's side shade and opened the mirror. Back when she had been on patrol years ago, she'd worn her hair in a ponytail or bun: a requirement. Now that she had more of a desk job, interviewing people on occasion—investigating—she let it hang unencumbered, traveling past her shoulders in straight strands.

She checked the right contact in her sky-blue eyes again. Putting contacts in at 4:50 A.M. was no easy task.

The day was just breaking over Alexandria, Virginia, the sun rising in the distant skyline above Washington, D.C. As a suburb of the nation's capital and a town still grasping ahold of the traditional charms of the South, Alexandria danced with an enticing double identity. Its rich colonial history compelled it to preserve most of its historical homes, boutique shops, and small markets—especially in Old Town Alexandria—yet modern mass transit systems snaked their way through the city and digital billboards dotted the highways.

Brooke stepped out of her car, stretching her long limbs in the humid July morning. *This is my moment*, she thought she had dreamed of this promotion more than any other job she'd ever had; it was the reason she had gone to the academy in the first place.

After spending the last four years investigating all types of crimes against people, Detective Hill was now the head of the Domestic Violence Unit—the DVU. True, she was the *only* detective within the DVU in their small division of the Fairfax County Police force, but it was what she had always wanted, particularly after watching her mom suffer at the hands of her father's abuse. As a child, she had vowed she would do whatever she could to make a difference in the world, and while this was not the big-city detective job she'd always wanted, it was a step. An important step.

As she walked into the building, she collided with Officer Nick Simons, her head colliding with his shoulder to be more precise. This was not the confident entrance she was hoping to make.

"Ouch," he said, rubbing his left shoulder.

Brooke tried to collect herself, patting down her hair and adjusting her lavender button-down shirt underneath her black blazer. "I'm so sorry, I didn't see you there."

"You didn't see me right in front of you? I get it; I'm hard to miss." He winked and raised a to-go cup in front of her. "Dang, Hill, I even brought you coffee for your big day. Or do I need to say, *Detective* Hill?"

Nick was not hard to miss—quite the opposite, actually. He was six-foot-one and encased in pure muscle. Even though he was originally from a small town in Ohio and had traveled extensively as the son of a dedicated Army dad, he could have doubled for a blond California surfer any day of the week. And Brooke knew he didn't even artificially highlight that magnificent hair of his.

They had met in the academy, and though there had always been an unspoken, smoldering attraction between the two, their relationship had remained platonic, even as inseparable as they had become. There was the drunk New Year's Eve kiss several years back, but nothing after that. Timing was never their thing, they would say.

"Like two passing ships," Nick muttered whenever the subject came up. One of them was always dating someone, and it was Nick's turn this time. As it crossed her mind the thought sliced Brooke's heart, though she would never admit that, even to herself.

"You got me coffee? You are the best," Brooke said, still adjusting herself after the collision. She couldn't tell if the blush she felt creeping up her face was from Nick or due to her absent-minded run-in. "And yes, on the job, it's gotta be 'Detective.'"

"Well, *Detective*, I wanted to wish you good luck on the first day of your big promotion. Hope you don't forget us little people still out on patrol." Nick winked again but added a smirk this time. Nick's career track had him on a collision course to make lieutenant someday soon.

Brooke's heart raced as she tried not to make eye contact. Her fleeting hope was that if she just avoided his eyes, she could forget about how gorgeous he was. Instead, she looked at the coffee cup now in her hand and allowed herself to fall into their usual flirtatious banter. "How could I ever forget you? You are like that pain I get in my back sometimes ... the one that takes me forever to get rid of."

Nick rolled his eyes. "I try to do something nice for someone ..."

"I appreciate it, thank you. How's Liv? Right? That's the new one's name?" Finally done fidgeting, she looked up at him and immediately regretted asking about his new flame.

"You know her name, Hill, and she's fine."

Of course she knew her name. A part of Brooke wanted this Liv person to go far, far away, never to return. But even if that happened, then what? They'd need a miracle to break through their long-time, weirdly flirtatious, status-quo friendship.

Nick raised his cup to cheers hers. "All right... got to hit the sheets. I'm wiped from last night. Good luck, Detective Hill. I'll text you later."

And he was off. She watched him walk away. Why hadn't she ever pursued anything with him? Yes, he was one of her best friends, but the chemistry between them was intense. She knew he felt it too. *There was no way he didn't, right?* Brooke shook her head as if to wobble the thought of them together from her mind.

"Stop staring at my ass!" Nick yelled as he opened the door to the parking lot. With a turn and a grin, he was gone.

"I can't tell if you two ever did get together if it'd be fireworks or if you'd end up killing one another." A voice came from behind Brooke, one she would know anywhere.

"Probably the latter," she said, turning.

The voice belonged to none other than recently retired Detective Benjamin Noble, her mentor and the outgoing head of the DVU. Benji was a short, stocky man with graying hair and an even grayer mustache—a mustache he had first started growing when he was in the academy some thirty-odd years ago. Somehow, he'd never shaven it off. "I'm a cop. I need a mustache. Watch any of the good '80s cop shows; all of them have mustaches," he told people.

"How you doing, kid? Nervous?" Benji cocked his head to the side, a look of concern spread across his face. Brooke knew he worried that by accepting this recent promotion that she had bitten off more than she could chew.

He had taught her in one of her first classes at the academy, and had remembered her name from years before, when he had responded to a domestic disturbance at her childhood home. An instant bond was created when he shared with her years later that he was the one who had rescued her and her little sister, Cassie, that night.

He was proud of the little five-year-old he'd met then, the one who had decided to dedicate her life to helping others at such a tender age. He lobbied hard for her to be placed in his division, and lobbied even harder to become her mentor. The minute Benji decided to retire, he had gone directly to Chief Anthony and told him he would be an idiot if he did not hire Brooke as his replacement. While he worried about her, he knew there was no better fit for this role.

"I just don't want to screw up. This is the whole reason I became a police officer." She looked to him for reassurance, her teeth pinching her bottom lip.

"You'll do great, kid. I would not have given my seal of approval if I thought you would mess up all my years of work," he said with a squeeze on her arm.

"Speaking of being your replacement, what are you doing here? Aren't you supposed to be retired at this very moment, old man? Sleeping in or something?" Brooke had no problem giving it back to Benji, almost as well as she took his teasing.

"Funny… but I thought I would hang around a bit this week— make sure you have everything you need."

"I can't tell if you are worried about me or worried I am actually going to mess up."

"A little bit of both." Benji grinned. "Actually, your first case came in last night. The Lieutenant and Officer Beal are waiting in my—I mean *your*—office to brief you. I wanted to be there with you for this first one."

"Why's that?" Brooke asked, giving him a puzzled look.

Benji's face turned serious, and she knew it must be bad, judging from the pain already evident in his eyes. His response almost sent her coffee to the floor.

"Because it's a lot like what happened to you and Cassie."

CHAPTER 3

When Brooke and Benji stepped through the door of her office, Lieutenant Adams and Officer Dan Beal were waiting for them in the chairs on the near side of the desk. To say it was an office would be an exaggeration—it was more like a dusty shoebox holding a desk, the two metal chairs, and an old filing cabinet crammed with papers. The smells of old cigar smoke and industrial-strength carpet cleaner filled her nose, which she wrinkled.

Officer Beal was one of the nicest colleagues Brooke had. Short, strapping, and tattooed-up, he sported a dark blond man-bun, which the department heads despised almost as much as the amount of ink blanketing his arms. The sight of her kind friend brought a smile to her face. Dan Beal was always the first one to volunteer for extra duty if it meant it would help a friend, someone known for literally giving people the shirt off his back and never thinking twice about it. If anyone was going to respond to a domestic disturbance, she would want it to be him.

"Detective Hill," he said with a salute and a smile as he stood up to greet her.

"Oh, would you stop? You ever going to cut off that ridiculous man-bun?" Brooke settled into her new desk and motioned for him to sit. She heard Lieutenant Adams chuckle. Benji remained standing, taking up an entire corner of the tiny room.

"You sound like my wife. I told Kat the minute we have a boy, it's as good as gone. Until that happens, forget it." Beal had three beautiful, golden-haired little girls with curls that bounced atop their heads and who frequently stopped by the station.

"Tell her what happened, Lieutenant," Benji said, rushing them along. Brooke couldn't tell if he was eager to get on with his day or anxious for her to hear what happened.

"You go ahead, Officer Beal. You were there," their boss directed.

"Right." Beal pulled out his notepad. "I responded to a domestic disturbance last night at 2100 hours. The address was 1516 Sherwood, right off English Ivy."

"Is that the new development, just built... what's it called?" Brooke fired up her laptop.

"Yep. Harbor Meadows. Took me a minute to figure out where I was responding to. Waze doesn't even have the street address in its system yet."

Brooke typed the address into the database that popped up on her screen. "No previous calls to police?"

"No. Apparently, the wife had threatened to call us before but never followed through."

This sent a chill down Brooke's spine, which nestled into her gut. She knew this song and dance all too well; she and Cassie lived it out for much of their early childhood. Even now, when she closed her eyes, she could hear their mother screaming at their father, again and again, threatening to call the cops on him... but never doing it.

She pressed on, focusing on her laptop. "Don and Ann Reese? Young couple, forty and thirty-six years old." Her lungs spasmed.

They were almost the same ages her parents had been when the worst-case scenario unfolded. She cleared her throat. "Any kids?"

"Yes, a boy and a girl. Conner, age five, and Emma, age four. Both children were home during the incident," Beal replied.

Brooke shot a glance at Benji, who gave her a sympathetic look. They were thinking the same thing: the kids were the exact ages as Brooke and Cassie when their lives crumbled around them.

Brooke finally looked Beal in the eyes, then placed her head into her hands. "Dan, please tell me they are safe."

"The kids and Ann are all safe. Don Reese is still being held, but he will be released today. Do you want me to continue, or do you need a moment?"

The room fell silent as Brooke collected her thoughts. Beal knew Brooke's story, as did everyone from their year at the police academy. Over pizza and beer one night early in training, she had shared with her little cohort—which included Nick Simmons and Dan Beal—the reason, at five years old, she decided to become a police officer.

"Detective?" Lieutenant Adams asked, a look of concern plastered itself across her face.

At least everyone is safe. This gave Brooke some solace. "I'm good. Tell me the details," she said, lifting her head.

"I was the first one to respond. Moore and Thomas followed shortly after. The wife, Ann Reese, answered the door. Her hair and shirt were wet, apparently from a glass of water Mr. Reese had thrown on her while they were arguing. He then allegedly threatened to kill her as she tried to call us while in the house, so she grabbed the kids and ran to a neighbor's house."

Beal cleared his throat before continuing. "Mr. Reese drove off before I got there. He didn't get very far. I got on the radio, and he was picked up about two miles away. I met him and the arresting officer at the county jail. The magistrate locked him up without bail 'till this morning and granted Mrs. Reese an emergency protective order. He's being charged with assault."

Brooke searched for something to write with. "Where do things stand now? Did you go back to the residence? How was Mrs. Reese?" Brooke's questions come out rapid-fire, fueled by her emotions. She rummaged through her papers and opened a drawer.

"Top left," whispered Benji from the corner of the room. Brooke grabbed the pen she spied and made a mental note to rearrange the entire desk later.

"Honestly? A little shell-shocked. She met me outside with a glass of bourbon in her hand, saying she didn't want the kids to see a police officer at the house. I advised her to go to court today to get the two-week extension for the protective order, and she said she would. She also said she had called her brother, who was driving down from Philadelphia at that moment to change the locks and passcodes for the house."

"OK. Do you think she understands the seriousness of this?"

"I don't know. She was in shock and worried about the kids. Apparently, Mr. Reese has a history of domestic violence... even though she's never called for help before."

Brooke nodded. "Did you tell her she should expect a visit from me?"

"I told her my very good friend just got promoted to head of DVU and would be reaching out today. She made a joke about wondering who would view that as a promotion." Beal smiled.

Brooke returned the smile, but it never reached her eyes. "Thanks."

The lieutenant jumped back in. "Go home and get some rest, Officer Beal. Detective Hill will look over the report and then reach out to Mrs. Reese."

Beal handed Brooke his paperwork, then rose to leave, following their boss through the doorway. After he'd turned the corner, Beal returned. "Brooke—I mean, Detective Hill—there is one more thing," he said as he looked over his shoulder to see if the LT was out of earshot.

"What's that?" Brooke glanced from Beal to Benji, wondering if Benji knew what bomb was about to be dropped.

"Mr. Reese did not just threaten to kill his wife. He threatened to burn the house down with her and the children inside. He's also being charged with threat to burn. After she ran out of the front door, she saw him with a gas can and a lighter in his hands."

Brooke felt her office walls shrink around her. She stared ahead blankly, lost in the painful memories of long ago.

Benji stepped forward from the corner, where he had been leaning up against the old filing cabinet. "You OK, kid?"

"Detective?" Beal asked from the doorway. The two remaining visitors glanced at one another.

Brooke took a deep breath in and blew it out before speaking. "I'm OK, guys. Thanks for letting me know. I'll read the report right now and contact Mrs. Reese."

Benji seemed the most concerned, but she waved away his look of apprehension. "Honestly, I'm good… Dan, go home and get some rest—like the lieutenant said; you look like crap."

Beal took his leave, giving her another mini salute to ease the tension. Benji remained, not quite sure what to do. "You want me to go or stay?"

Brooke looked at the man who'd sat in this office before her. He was more than a mentor; he was family. He and his wife, Carol, had taken Brooke, Cassie, and Aunt T—her mother's sister who became their guardian when their parents passed—into their fold, including them in many Sunday dinners and holidays. But right now, she needed him to go.

"Don't get soft on me—I'm OK. This case is going to hit very close to home; we both know that. But if this is my career now, I'm going to have to get used to it. Honestly, I am fine. Go." Brooke mustered up the best fake smile she could, rising from her chair.

"Kicked out of my own office," Benji said with a wink as he shuffled toward the door.

Brooke put her hands on her hips. "It's my office now."

"Fair enough. I'll be in tomorrow to grab some files. Remember, kid, I am only a phone call away. You sure you're OK?"

Brooke threw the pen at him. It hit the door frame to the left of his arm. "Stop worrying. I'm fine. I'd tell you if I wasn't."

"All right. Carol is making her famous meatloaf on Sunday. You better not be late."

Brooke closed the door behind him and then sat back down, the police report in her hand. It felt as if the paper itself was on fire. She never imagined her first case would carry so many similarities to her story. She read the first page, then put it down. She needed a breather. She needed to talk to the only other person who could understand. She needed Cassie.

CHAPTER 4

Brooke bent her left elbow and looked at the time on her smartwatch. It was just after 8:00 A.M. She was almost certain Cassie would still be sleeping, or maybe even just going to bed. Still trying to make it as the Broadway star she knew she was destined to be, Cassie worked a series of waitressing and bartending jobs. Since her little sister hustled in the city that never sleeps, Brooke normally waited until afternoon to call, but she was desperate to talk to her.

Ironically, she didn't need to wait. Her phone started ringing with a FaceTime call, from Cassie herself. Startled, Brooke picked up right away. "What's wrong?"

"I can't just call my big sister on the first day of her big, new job? I set an alarm and everything." Cassie smiled, and the dimples in her cheeks seemed to kiss the screen. It was an endearing smile that attracted others like moths to light. She was still lying in bed in her ragged, high school PE T-shirt, but it didn't matter—Cassie was gorgeous. Though Brooke and Cassie looked similar—everyone could tell they were sisters—Cassie had been blessed with beautiful brown ringlet curls, which cascaded to her shoulders. Her blue eyes, like Brooke's, sat in mesmerizing contrast to her dark hair.

From the moment she left the womb, Cassie Hill had been a force to be reckoned with. Their mother had liked to joke that Cassie was not pulled out; she strutted out. With her larger-than-life personality, Cassie had always been destined for stardom. It came as no surprise when, the minute she graduated from high school, she had gathered all of her belongings and made a "do not pass go" beeline to New York City.

"Aw, Cass, that was sweet. Thank you." Brooke took a sip of her now-lukewarm coffee. There was no denying that something was occupying her mind, and Cassie picked up on it immediately.

"Hold up. Something is wrong; I can see it in your eyes." Cassie sat up in bed so she could direct her full attention to her sister.

"I'm fine, honest." Brooke glanced nervously around her desk, suddenly hesitant to say too much. A moment ago, she was craving her sister's care. Now, she wanted to shield Cassie from the emotional ride she was experiencing.

"Liar. Before we get off the phone, you're going to tell me."

Brooke sighed. "Deal. How are you? How was the audition?" Brooke gripped the role of older sister and nurturer, determined to never let go, and Cassie relented to the routine.

As her sister complained about how unreasonable the director was, Nick appeared, leaning against the doorframe to Brooke's shoebox office. Sensing someone was gazing at her, Brooke looked up.

"I ran into Beal," he mouthed. "You OK?"

"Who's there? Who are you looking at?" Cassie asked. Brooke turned the phone so Cassie could see Nick standing in doorway.

"Looking good, Officer Simons. I should have known you would be lurking around my sister's new office. Wait, B, is *this* your office? It's awful! You have *got* to redecorate."

"Hi, gorgeous. Her office isn't so bad. Desk seems sturdy," Nick said with a wink at Brooke.

"Oh my gosh! Would you stop flirting with my sister and get on with it? I don't know how many more years I can take of this!" Cassie giggled on the other end of the phone.

Nick grinned back, used to the banter. "I'm leaving. Just stopped to see if Brooke was OK." He peered at her, looking past the outstretched phone. "Are you?"

"I'm fine." Brooke knew she did not sound convincing.

"I knew something was wrong!" Cassie yelled. "Turn me back around."

"We need to work on your poker face, Hill," Nick said.

"I'm fine. I'm not going to fall to pieces. If I was, I would have already. And I thought you were heading home. And by the way, *you* are the one who gave it away," Brooke said, ignoring Cassie for the moment.

"Sorry. OK, I'll check on you in a bit. Love you, Hill," Nick said as he turned to leave.

"Love you, too, Simons. Thanks for checking on me."

He was gone. Cassie had gone silent, but clearly, she had many things to say. Brooke closed her eyes briefly. When she opened them, her sister was still staring at her through the phone. Then Cassie blinked rapidly, trying to make her point. "That man wants to sleep with you. He is just waiting for you to make a move."

Brooke rolled her eyes. "Yeah, OK. Can we talk about something else?"

"How about we start with what is bothering you so much so that Officer Hottie had to come back in and check on you?"

Brooke took a deep breath and another sip of her coffee. "I got my first case as soon as I walked in this morning."

"Wow! They really don't give you much breathing room on the first day." Cassie had jumped out of bed and was now pacing around her small Brooklyn apartment that she shared with three roommates.

"No, they don't. Dan Beal was the one who responded, and he was waiting for me with the lieutenant when I walked in. I should have known it was going to be bad when all three stayed to brief me in person."

"Your boss, Man-bun, and Benji? This must be bad." As Cassie settled back into her bed, Brooke took another gulp of her cooling coffee.

"It is going to be a really hard case to work. It has some pretty eerie comparisons to what happened with us, right down to everyone's ages. The only difference so far is that the oldest child is a boy."

Brooke paused and stared at her sister, waiting for her response. Cassie stopped adjusting her comforter and avoided looking at Brooke's image on the screen. "Are they safe?" Cassie asked quietly.

"Everyone is safe—for the time being. The mom was able to get the kids out of the house and the dad was arrested."

Cassie took a deep breath and pulled one of her curls, then set it loose to coil like a slinky once again. "Well, there is another really big difference then… everyone is still alive."

CHAPTER 5

Cassie was right on that point. Everyone in the Reeses' case was still alive. The same could not be said for their own family.

"Remember why you got into this," Cassie continued. "You wanted to make sure that what happened to us and to Mom would never happen to someone else—remember that. This is not going to be the first case you'll have that reminds you of our story."

Cassie was right again. Her last sentence would have seemed harsh on paper, but spoken with love over the phone, it brought encouragement. Brooke groaned, leaning back in her desk chair, nearly falling off because of how old and rickety it was. "I know you're right," she said, steadying herself with a hand on her desk. "It's just some of the details are hard to handle."

"Like what?" Cassie propped herself up again.

Brooke closed her eyes and put a closed fist to her mouth, bracing herself to tell her sister. "Cass, when the mom ran out of the house with her kids, she turned around, and in the dad's hand was a gas can. He was also holding a lighter."

"Oh my—" Like Brooke, Cassie put her hand over her mouth and gasped.

There are moments in everyone's life they wish they could forget. *That night*—when Brooke was five years old—was one of those nights.

It was the yelling she always recalled first, the sound of both parents screaming at full volume. Frightened by the noise, Cassie had sneaked down the second-floor hallway and climbed into Brooke's twin bed, snuggling up next to her big sister. For nearly two hours, they hid under Brooke's Minnie Mouse sheets and duvet with their flashlights, holding hands.

A few minutes after ten o'clock, their mother ran into Brooke's room, a look of terror spread across her flushed face. Her eyes were wide, and her short, medium-brown hair looked disheveled, as if she hadn't blown it dry after a shower. Her cheeks were stained with tear tracks. The image wasn't something either daughter would ever forget. "Girls, we have to go. Now!"

Cassie and Brooke scrambled from the blankets and raced out of Brooke's room, holding only their Cabbage Patch dolls and each other's hands. But as the girls reached the safety of the front lawn and breathed in the chilly outside air, they realized their mother was no longer behind them. When they turned, they saw their father with a red gas can in one hand and a long candle lighter in the other. Their mother stood just beyond the doorway, still inside the house. That's when young Brooke realized there'd been a specific odor, which her little nose had detected as she ran, wafting through the house from which she and Cassie had just escaped. The house smelled like the garage always did after Dad mowed the yard.

In that instant, the foyer, then a few seconds later most of the downstairs level of the house, went up in flames, the rush of the inferno taking both of their parents with it.

"B, are you sure you're OK? Maybe you give this case to Benji. It can be his one last hurrah before retiring." Cassie's deep concern was etched throughout her furrowed brows and pinched lips. Even her dimples had disappeared.

Brooke shook her head. "No, I need to do this. It's been over two decades. It's fine; I'll be OK. After all, like you said, this is the reason I became a cop. This is my *why*."

"How about I come down this weekend? I don't have any real auditions lined up this week, and I am sure I can get someone to take my shifts at the bar."

"Cass, I'm not in a crisis. I just know this case is going to be difficult."

Cassie rolled her blue eyes. "I know you're not in crisis. *Yet*. But I also know you better than anyone. You're going to take this case very personally. I just want to be there for you, and… I miss you."

"I miss you too. I might be working all weekend, so let's just touch base as the week goes on." Brooke tried for a compromise.

"Is working all weekend code for spending time with Nick?" Cassie winked, trying to lighten the mood.

"Very funny. No, working all weekend is code for probably working all weekend. Besides, he's seeing someone." Brooke realized she needed this levity, too, the fiery memories continuing to flash through her mind. So she egged on her sister with more information about Nick's newest girlfriend. "Her name is Liv."

It didn't work. "Heard all this before," Cassie said with an air of nonchalance. "All right, well, let me know. I could also use some of Carol's home cooking." Cassie was referring to Benji's wife's famous Sunday meals.

"Sounds good. I gotta get back to reading this report. I'll call you later."

"I love you, B." Cassie blew her a kiss.

"Love you, too, Cass." Brooke waved back.

After hanging up with her sister, Brooke looked again at the stack of papers, the report summary staring at her from the top. *Well, there's no time like the present.* She grabbed the paperwork and began reading.

———

Forty-five minutes later, Brooke was in the women's restroom, splashing water onto her face. The story and its details had caused another flood of traumatic childhood memories. She needed to compose herself before calling Mrs. Reese.

"Oh, there you are." June, the dispatcher, came up next to her. Hearing June's British, Mary Poppins-like voice was soothing. She mothered all the officers at the station—always serving as a much-needed source of comfort. "Are you alright?" she asked, putting a hand on Brooke's back.

"Yeah, I'm fine. Thanks. Just got a little sleepy; that's all." Brooke turned to face the silver-haired woman whose wrinkled face smiled with a warmth that rivaled that of Mr. Rogers. Brooke smiled at the thought of Mary Poppins and Mr. Rogers together. She could use those two famous, whimsical nurturers right about now.

"I was paging you, but you didn't pick up. Thought I would take a walk to see if I could find you. You have a phone call."

"Sure. I'll be right out. Who is my mystery caller?" Brooke grabbed a paper towel to dry her hands.

"I believe she said her name was Ann Reese."

CHAPTER 6

Before picking up the desk phone to talk to Mrs. Reese, Brooke sat down and glanced at her cell phone. Notifications for two missed calls from her Aunt Talia and five text messages stared up at her.

The first text was from Cassie: *I decided I'm coming down on Friday and staying till Monday. Calling work later today. You can't stop me.... don't bother trying.*

I should have seen that coming, Brooke thought, shaking her head.

The next message was from Jacs, her fierce, red-headed best friend: *B, Cass just texted me. Sorry your first day is starting with this. Drinks later?*

And one from Aunt T: *I just called you twice, call me when you have a second. Good luck on your first day, love! So proud of you. I know your mom would be too.* Any mention of Brooke's mom brought usually brought a thin veil of tears, especially now. She dabbed the corner of her eyes with a tissue she swiped from the box on her desk, feeling grateful that Benji—or, more likely, the cleaning crew—had left some.

The next one was from Benji. It always took Brooke by surprise when Benji texted—technology was not his thing. *There's an emergency bottle of bourbon at the bottom of the filing cabinet in case you need it.*

And finally, she opened a meme from Nick. It showed RuPaul saying, "Get it, Gurl." It made Brooke giggle, breaking the heaviness she had been feeling for the past hour.

With a deep breath, Brooke picked up her office phone. "Hello, Mrs. Reese, this is Detective Brooke Hill."

"Hi, Detective Hill." Brooke could hear the shakiness in Mrs. Reese's voice and wondered if this poor woman had slept at all last night. "I know Officer Beal said you would be calling, but I was about to head to the courthouse and wanted to speak to you before I did that. Is this a good time, or should I call back?" Mrs. Reese's trembling voice sent an electric shock down Brooke's spine, giving her goosebumps on her arms—it reminded her of her mom's tone when she had tried to comfort her and Cassie. Brooke also detected an echo as Mrs. Reese spoke, and she wondered if the woman was in a bathroom. Experience had taught her that most mothers did anything and everything to help prevent their children from experiencing more pain—or in this case, from hearing their conversation.

"I just finished reading Officer Beal's report and was about to call you to let you know I'm coming over. How are you holding up, Mrs. Reese?" Brooke looked around again for something to write with.

"Please, call me Ann. I've had better days." Brooke could hear sniffling on the other end.

"So you're going to the courthouse today for the extension of the protective order? You have till Wednesday to do so." After locating another long-lost pen in the drawer, Brooke fiddled with the papers in front of her.

Ann laughed nervously. "I'm afraid if I don't do it now, I'll lose my nerve."

"I understand. Did Officer Beal walk you through some of the process last night so you know what to expect as the case unfolds?" Brooke took notes on the back of the case file as they spoke.

"I'm sure he did, but honestly, I think I'm still in shock. The paperwork he gave me when he came back last night is still sitting on the kitchen table. I'm hiding in the bathroom so my children don't overhear."

Bingo. Brooke's first correct deduction gave her a burst of confidence.

"That's understandable. This whole thing—your experience—is overwhelming. I'm here, Ann. My job is to make sure that you are OK and have what you need. I'm your new best friend."

"Thank you," Ann said as she started to sob. "I just… can't believe this… is my life."

"Let's just take it one step at a time. Your first step is to go to the courthouse and get an extension for that protective order."

"And after that?"

"Well, you are going to need to hire a lawyer. At least for future protective order stuff."

"Do you think I will need two? One for a divorce and one for the criminal stuff?"

Brooke was taken aback. She had planned to stress to Ann that she should not let her husband back in the house, but she was not expecting Ann to throw the "*D* word" around quite yet.

"It's possible. The easiest thing to do is go within one law firm. Fortunately, we live right outside of D.C., so the choices are endless. What's your email address? I can send you a few options."

Her crying had slowed. "Thank you. I really appreciate it." Ann gave Brooke her email address before asking, "Do you know when my husband is being released from jail?"

"Let me check. Hang on one second." Brooke did a quick search of the database on her laptop. "It appears he has already been released."

Silence.

"Ann?" Nothing. "Mrs. Reese?" Nothing again. "Ann, are you still there?" Brooke willed herself not to panic.

Ann's voice was quiet. "I'm sorry. I'm here. It's just…" She trailed off.

"You're scared."

"I'm more than scared—I'm terrified. He's going to kill me."

Brooke closed her eyes. "I'm not going to let that happen. This is my job—to help you, and to keep you and your children safe." Brooke tried her best to sound reassuring, but her heart rate had ratcheted up, and she felt a bead of sweat slide down her armpit onto her torso.

Ann sniffled. "I appreciate that, but I worry that no one can really protect me."

Brooke re-opened her eyes. "I understand how you feel. But he is not going to hurt you anymore. Go get the protective order extension. Cross that one thing off your list today. I believe Officer Beal said your brother is coming to change your locks and alarm system passcode; is that correct?" Brooke leaned forward on her desk. She was hoping she was giving off an air of confidence with her tone. She needed Ann to believe that Brooke could keep her safe. *Or is it me who needs to believe this?*

"Yes, he drove through the night and got here a few hours ago. He's changing the locks and the passwords to the alarm system and cameras. My husband works in IT, and the house is wired top to bottom—cameras everywhere. I don't even know where to begin."

"I think after your brother is done, you should have the house swept by a private investigator. Make sure there is no way for your husband to be watching you or listening to you. Hold on, Ann. Give me a second." Brooke hit the hold button on the landline office phone. She opened a browser and did a quick search. After typing out another email, she put the receiver back to her ear and hit button to open the line again. "I just sent you a list of people who do this, and I will also make contact with the officers who patrol that area, both during the day and night. They'll keep their antennas up."

Ann sighed. "Thank you."

"I know this is scary, but you've got this. Go to the courthouse, and then call me back. Let me give you my cell number." Brooke waited to rattle off the digits as Ann searched for a paper and pen in her bedroom.

"Thank you, Detective Hill."

"Ann, I am so sorry this happened. I'll wait for your phone call later today… please call me once you leave the courthouse."

They hung up and Brooke looked at the clock hanging on the wall above the door. The hour hand was just hitting 10:00 a.m. on her first day of work. If this was just the morning, Brooke wondered how the rest of her day would go—or her career.

CHAPTER 7

T he rest of Brooke's morning was relatively quiet. She spent most of the time trying to brush up on two cases Benji had just finished, cases that she would now be the point person for in court. One was a repeat domestic disturbance call, where the boyfriend and girlfriend took turns being the victim, and the other was a case Benji had worked on for years—the protective order was due to be renewed, and the plaintiff was contesting it. Neither was quite as dramatic as the new case that had landed on her desk.

When three o'clock rolled up on the clock on the wall, Brooke realized she had never stopped for lunch. Just as she was contemplating what she would get out of the vending machine, June called. "Brooke, you have a phone call. It's Greg Levine. Should I patch him through?"

"Ugh." Brooke rolled her eyes, though no one was there to see it. Greg Levine was a criminal defense attorney in northern Virginia and the most abrasive man she had ever met. Early in her career, she had to testify, and he cross-examined her. Brooke had been left scarred; she could still hear him saying, "I'm sorry, Officer Hill, you *think*, or you *know*?"

"Would you like me to send him to your voicemail?" June chuckled. No one liked this guy, not even Mrs. Mary Poppins-Rogers.

"No, I might as well get it over with. Put him through. Thanks, June." As the phone beeped, Brooke took a deep breath, fixed her hair out of habit, and picked up. *Here we go.*

"Mr. Levine, it's been a while."

"Officer Hill, or should I say *Detective* Hill? How the heck are you?" Brooke sat forward in her desk chair—why in the world was he being so nice to her?

"I'm doing pretty well…thanks. To what do I owe the pleasure?" *I definitely need my guard up for this call.* Through the line she could smell some type of impending ambush.

"Can't a defense attorney just call the newest detective and welcome her aboard? I'm sure Detective Noble told you what a close friendship we developed over the years."

And there was the first lie. A close friendship was not how Benji would describe his interactions with Greg Levine—a thorn in his side was more like it. Brooke stayed silent and waited for Greg to say more.

"Right, well actually, there is a reason I'm calling. I just signed a new client this morning, and it appears he was brought in by one of the officers at your station. It was a domestic violence incident that occurred last night. Hang on… I can get the name for you." Greg said.

Crap, Brooke thought. She knew right away who his new client was, but still, she prayed. *Please don't say Don Reese.*

"Here it is. I'm not sure if you have had contact with the wife yet. Her name is Ann Reese. Husband's name is Don."

"And you represent Don Reese now; is that what you're telling me?" A sense of dread loomed over her, pushing down on her shoulders from somewhere above. She rubbed her forehead, feeling a migraine coming on.

"Yes. He was released from jail this morning, and I was his first phone call. He just left my office," Greg said.

Brooke again remained silent, still not sure why Greg felt the need to call and tell her this information.

"Have you spoken to the wife yet?" he asked.

"Mr. Levine…" Brooke tapped her third pen of the day against the desk in agitation.

"Oh, please, call me Greg."

"OK, *Greg*, I am not going to comment on an ongoing police investigation. I have to be honest; I am not even sure why you're calling me."

"This is a simple courtesy," Greg said smugly. "I am letting you know that I am representing Don Reese."

"Great, thanks for the call. Anything else?" Brooke began rearranging the papers on her desk with the nervous energy flowing through her body.

"Brooke, I don't think you understand. I'm representing Don Reese, and I'm going to ask for the first offender's disposition and get it."

Brooke hated how confident he sounded—it made her nervous. She had to take the offensive position. "It's Detective Hill."

Brooke knew the first offender disposition was given to anyone who had committed their first offense. If Don Reese stayed in legal line for two years, then this incident would be erased from his record. And that was the kicker—as long as Don avoided police interaction, he could still torment his wife and kids.

"OK, well, good luck with that." Brooke hoped she sounded confident, but if Greg could see her, he'd see the worry lines stretching across her forehead. The chance of Don Reese getting this deal was high—he had no previous record, and the neighborhood in which the Reeses lived told Brooke that neither resources nor civic reputation would be issues.

"Do you know if Mrs. Reese has obtained counsel yet… or what she is doing with the protective order?"

"Greg, again, I am not commenting on any ongoing investigation." *Rein it in, Brooke. You're starting to sound agitated.*

"Thank you for your time, *Detective*, and congratulations on the promotion. You have some big shoes to fill." Brooke couldn't tell if he was being condescending or not.

As she slammed the phone down, her cell phone buzzed with simultaneous text messages. The first was from Jacs, asking if she wanted to meet for drinks later at their favorite drag bar; the second was from Ann Reese:

Hi Detective Hill. Thank you so much for this morning. I'm back home and was wondering if you could give me a call when you have a chance. I tried the station, but they said you were unavailable. I hope texting you is OK.

Brooke called Ann immediately, and the woman picked up after the first ring. "Hi, Detective Hill. Thank you for calling me back so quickly."

"No problem, Ann. Did you go to the courthouse?"

"I did. I got an extension for the protective order for two weeks. They said in two weeks we will need to appear in court to get the permanent one. I called two law firms from the list, and my brother is still here, changing the locks and taking down cameras. I also called the first private investigator from the list you sent, and he is coming the day after tomorrow to sweep the house while the kids are at school."

"That's great, Ann. I'm proud of you for accomplishing all that today. How are you feeling?" Brooke leaned back in her chair, impressed that Ann had gotten as much done as she said she would.

"I was fine until my brother handed me a summons for the criminal charges from last night. The hearing is set for Friday. And then

I checked my voicemail—I had one from CPS and one from Greg Levine, who is my husband's defense attorney, apparently." And with that, Ann started to cry.

I hate that man, thought Brooke. "I know this is hard, Ann. What did the voicemails say?" Brooke grabbed her pad of paper and the latest pen to take notes.

"CPS said they will need to come out and meet with me because the children were witnesses to the abuse. I just... I'm so upset that child protective services was called on me." She sounded like she was trying hard to keep it together. Every few words changed in volume, and Brooke had to strain to hear some of them over the phone.

"They were not called on you. They were called on him. Because of what *he* did. Did they say when they are coming out?"

"Tomorrow at noon." Ann blew her nose.

"OK." Brooke placed Ann on speaker and looked at the calendar on her phone. "I can swing by at the same time. I want to hear what they have to say, and I can be there to help."

"Thank you."

"What did Greg Levine say?" Brooke's stomach lurched at the mention of his name.

"I didn't call him back yet. I wasn't sure if I should be speaking to him, but his voicemail said we needed to work out a way for Don to get some personal belongings and see the children. Can you believe that? After what he did, he now wants to see the children?"

"Ann, I can't give you any legal advice, but what I can say is do *not* call Greg Levine back. Wait until you have counsel, then have them communicate with him. Do not take his calls."

"OK, I won't." Brooke could hear the faint sound of traffic as Ann spoke. She must have stepped outside, not wanting the children to overhear her conversation.

"I'll be over around noon tomorrow with CPS. We can go over any other questions you might have then."

"Thank you, Detective Hill. I really appreciate your help." The promise of having Brooke there when CPS arrived seemed to give Ann a bit of solace.

"I'm happy to help. Please, call me Brooke. And try to get some rest."

"I will. Thank you, Brooke."

As they hung up, Brooke glanced up at the clock. It was 5:00 P.M., and her shift officially ended. Her phone buzzed as if the person on the other end had been watching the clock, waiting for the workday to be finished. Nick's name popped up with a new text: *Day 1 down. Time for a drink?*

Brooke couldn't help but smile.

CHAPTER 8

"**W**ait, which one was Summer?" Jacs downed her second gin and tonic. They were perched at their usual red linoleum bar-top table at Freddie's Gay Bar, and Violet, their favorite drag queen, was serving their drinks. Her makeup was flawless, though heavy-handed, and her purple wig was an obvious nod to her name. Dressed in an '80s-style, flesh-colored tube top and leather pants, Violet vied for the best outfit of the evening.

Jacs, Brooke, and Nick had all arrived for happy hour, with Jacs still dressed in her "corporate gear," which she wore for her job at the U.S. Senate. Her black suit and teal blouse highlighted her green eyes, but not as much as her shoulder-length red hair. Her cheeks were growing pinker with each passing minute, likely from the alcohol.

Jacs and Brooke were partaking in one of their favorite pastimes— teasing Nick about his not-so-stellar dating history. "Wasn't she the one with the weird bangs?" Brooke asked.

Jacs laughed. "Wait, she was the one who worked at Victoria's Secret, right?"

The two friends cracked up, nearly spilling their drinks.

"You two suck." Nick took a swig of his beer. The girls had been at the guessing game for a solid ten minutes, and it was clearly wearing on Nick's nerves, but he answered them anyway. "She's the one who threw her keys at me when we broke up."

"Oh!" Brooke and Jacs said in unison.

"Didn't you duck?" Brooke asked. They were all laughing at this point.

"Yup, and the keys hit the picture behind my head, breaking the glass," Nick said. "I don't remember what I said that set her off. And she was not happy to see me when I strolled up to her window last year after I pulled her over for speeding."

"I bet!" Brooke and Jacs again responded in unison, then broke into another fit of laughter, causing Jacs to snort. This was rewarded with a smile from Nick.

"I don't remember… did you end up giving her the ticket?" Jacs asked.

"Of course I did! I looked it up and cited her with the exact amount it cost to get that picture repaired!"

More laughter. Violet came by, and Jacs ordered another round. Brooke gave her a knowing look, and Jacs rolled her eyes. "Relax! This will be it. We all have to get up and adult tomorrow. So how was the first day, Detective?"

"Rough, but I suppose that will be par for the course with this job." As she said this, Nick squeezed her leg underneath the table. This did not go unnoticed by Jacs, who gave Brooke the side eye.

"You want to talk about it?" Jacs asked.

"Not really. At least not in any more detail than Cassie has already told you." Brooke tilted her head away from Jacs while looking her up and down, narrowing her eyes at her target.

"Don't be mad at her! She was just worried." Jacs downed the last of her drink.

Brooke straightened up in her chair. "I'm not mad. This case is a lot like what we went through as kids, but that was twenty-six years ago."

Now Jacs and Nick were the ones to exchange looks.

Nick leaned forward. "Look, just promise us something. If it gets to be too much, you say something." Brooke opened her mouth in protest, but he continued, not allowing her to talk yet. "I'm not saying hand off the case to someone else. I'm just saying…"

As his phone began to ring, Nick trailed off, and a broad smile spread across his face. Brooke knew that smile well, and a pang of jealousy crept across her heart. She could guess who was calling.

Nick stood up. "I'll be right back."

After Nick was out of earshot, Jacs stared hard at Brooke from across the table.

"Don't," was all Brooke said as she watched Nick walk away.

"Don't what?"

"Don't say what we both know you want to say." With their twenty-year friendship, they could read each other's thoughts. Brooke turned to face her best friend.

"He's waiting on you to make the move, and if you aren't careful, you're going to lose him to one of these women. I don't know if you can live with that kind of regret. And spare me the *I-don't-want-to-ruin-our-friendship* face. I'm tired of watching him undress you with his eyes and you looking at him like a love-struck teenager."

Brooke's eyes widened. "Wow! Don't hold back, Jacs."

"I love you, but you are being stupid. So is he, but as a male, he is genetically inferior, so he has an excuse. You don't." Jacs glanced at a TV screen overhead as if making a hard stop with her statement.

Brooke smirked, mostly at the situation itself. *Maybe Jacs has a point.*

Nick walked back in. "Sorry about that."

"How's Liv?" Brooke asked.

"Annoyed." Nick seemed to feel the same way, based on the tone of his voice. "I told her I was out and wasn't going to come over tonight. She didn't like that." Violet walked by and Nick stopped her to order a round of tequila shots.

"No! I cannot be hungover for my second day on the job!" Brooke protested.

"Come on, Brookie! I'll let you lick the salt off of me." Nick winked. Jacs practically choked on her drink.

Brooke relented, mostly to keep Jacs from saying anything embarrassing. "Fine. But only one. And no licking."

He smiled. "Only one."

Four drinks and two tequila shots later, the threesome was heading out the door of the bar. Jacs parted ways with them on the sidewalk, leaving Nick and Brooke alone together under the glow of Freddie's neon lights.

"You drive or Uber?" he asked.

"Uber. You?"

"Same. Want to share one? My treat." Nick had a look on his face that Brooke could not quite make out. They lived on opposite sides of Alexandria; it didn't make sense to split an Uber, and Brooke knew Nick knew that. *Unless…*

"We go in opposite directions, Nick. You really have that much to drink?" She peered into his eyes and almost didn't come back out. Blinking, she cleared her throat.

"I did not. And we don't have to go in opposite directions all the time, Brooke. It might be nice if we went in the same direction for once." He looked at her with now hooded eyes, and Brooke realized he meant every word he was saying. He very much wanted her to read between the lines.

"Nick—"

Brooke was cut off by the ringing of Nick's cell phone. Without a word to her, he tapped the green phone icon right away.

"Hey, babe," Nick said, turning his back on Brooke.

Brooke's mouth dropped open. *I'm not sticking around for this.* Not wanting to wait for an Uber, she walked to the main street, found a lone cab, and gave the driver her home address. The taxi smelled like cabbage, and she stewed in the back seat as the driver turned his car around and drove in the opposite direction of where Nick lived. Her heart broke as she became just another passing ship in his night—again.

CHAPTER 9

At noon the next day, Brooke was on her way to the Reeses' residence. It had been a slow-moving start to the morning, no doubt courtesy of the tequila from the night before, and Brooke had done her best to disregard Nick's texts for the past twelve hours:

I just went by your office. Where r you?

You can't stay mad at me forever. You love me too much.

As she drove toward Harbor Meadows, she ignored his continued messages. She could not believe he was acting so cavalier about what he'd offered last night—unless he genuinely did not remember it, and Brooke had a hard time believing he didn't.

On an emotional ride that took her from one high to the next low, Brooke had thought of nothing else but Nick over the past several hours. His words, the look in his eyes. His *arms*. They were all captivating, and she would never admit it, but she *had* been looking at his butt yesterday when he jokingly called her out on it.

What made her fingers grip the steering wheel the most was the knowledge that he was right; she couldn't stay mad at him. But she was going to for now, at least until she figured out the right words to say, or until she knew how she'd be able to protect her heart from any future disappointment surely to come.

Maybe Cassie and Jacs were right about everything—she couldn't stop wondering what would have happened if Nick's new love interest hadn't called, intruding on their moment on the sidewalk. *But everything happens for a reason, right?* The problem was that she wasn't sure what the universe was trying to tell her about all of this.

Her cell phone rang and brought her back to the present. It was Aunt Talia.

"I gave up waiting for you to call," Aunt T said in a mock-scolding tone.

Brooke smiled. She could picture Aunt T, sitting in her sun-filled kitchen, both legs propped up on the windowsill. Her toffee-colored hair would be pulled back into a low ponytail, her glasses sitting just on the edge of her nose. She had given up her glamorous single life in San Francisco to move back to Springfield, Virginia, to take care of her two young nieces, a sacrifice Brooke did not fully appreciate until she had recently turned the same age Aunt T had been when the woman took guardianship of her and Cassie. She just couldn't imagine doing anything like that in her own life.

"Hi, Aunt T! I didn't forget; it's just been a whirlwind day or two," Brooke said, glancing at the car's navigation system, which could only take her so far since the new street the Reeses lived on wasn't in her GPS, either.

"I figured. I just wanted to check in and see how the first day went." Brooke heard a distant meow from her aunt's beloved elderly cat, Cookie.

"It was pretty good, just busy, and I'm exhausted. Have you talked to Cassie?"

"No, why?" Aunt T said, sounding somewhat alarmed. Everyone was always worried about Cassie—partly because she was the youngest, and partly because some people felt she had not fully grown up yet.

"No reason, really. She was thinking about coming down this weekend." As she lied, Brooke bit her lip. She was testing the waters to see if Cassie had reached out to tell their aunt about the Reese case.

"That means I will hear from her Friday morning, knowing Cassie. OK, love. I won't keep you. I know you are busy. I just wanted to say I am so proud of you and that I was thinking about you." The sentences tumbled out in quick succession. *Aunt T must be able to tell I'm distracted.*

"Thanks, Aunt T. I'll call you back later—I promise."

Remembering the directions Beal had given her once she entered the still-under-construction neighborhood, Brooke pulled up to the Reeses' house. It was a beautiful Craftsman-style residence set in a seven-home cul-de-sac, the houses all packed together. The low-pitched roof and exposed beams were beautiful, especially against the brown cedar singles and white trim. The wide-open front porch was held up by the signature columns of the style, and Brooke pictured two kids running through the front doors at night, with a young mother racing behind them, urging them forward. She shook her head to rid herself of the image.

After parking in the driveway, she exited her Camry, straightening her cream-colored dress shirt and making sure it was still neatly tucked into her navy slacks.

Ann Reese greeted Brooke at the door, before she even had had a chance to knock. "Detective Hill, it's so nice to meet you."

Instantly, Brooke was struck by the warmth Mrs. Reese exuded. Her medium brown hair was piled high on her head in a messy bun, and she wore black leggings and a long-sleeved George Washington University t-shirt with t. Without makeup, she bore a striking resemblance to Brooke's mother George Washington University they shared the same pinched nose and thin mouth. The realization gave Brooke a moment of pause.

"Hi, Ann. It's nice to put a face to the name. Has CPS shown up?" Brooke asked as she shook Ann's hand.

"Yes, the woman is looking through my refrigerator. Any ideas why she's searching in there?" Ann led Brooke inside.

"She wants to make sure you have enough food for the kids."

"Oh, right... that makes sense. I'm not thinking clearly." Ann gave a weak chuckle that fell between them, lost in the vanilla-scented air, courtesy of an air freshener Brooke spied plugged into an outlet in the foyer.

Ann led Brooke into a massive kitchen, where she was greeted by Diane Spense of Child Protective Services. Brooke vaguely recognized her from past run-ins during their respective careers, and they traded pleasantries.

All three women sat at Ann's long wooden kitchen table to discuss the circumstances of two nights ago. Before they started, Brooke apologized to Ann for having to rehash the traumatic event. "I know this is the last thing you want to talk about, and I really wish this was the last time you'll ever have to tell the tale, but it won't be. I'm so sorry." She squeezed Ann's hand.

Ann forced a smile. "It's OK. Every time I share the story, it gets a little easier, and it gives me a bit more strength knowing I had the courage to get out. And then get the story out, too, I guess."

"You are brave, Mrs. Reese. Don't let anyone tell you otherwise," Diane said.

After explaining some general backstory leading up to the scariest parts of the night in question, the women stood up, and Ann guided them through the house, pointing to where the specific events had happened and where the children were in relation to all of it. Her voice broke when she opened the door to her daughter's bedroom and showed them the bed in which she had found both children hiding. Brooke's stomach clenched, but she kept her resolve.

"Have you had any contact with your husband?" Diane asked.

"No. And I got the extension for the protective order," Ann replied.

"Good. Mrs. Reese, there will be an investigation into child abuse and neglect because of the events of that night. I want to be perfectly clear: the investigation is on your husband, *not you*. However, should you ever let him back into the house while there is a protective order in place, we will be having a very different conversation." Diane handed one of her cards to both Ann and Brooke and said she would be in touch.

Ann closed the front door after Diane walked out and looked at Brooke. "That was hard to hear." She took a deep breath. "Can I get you a cup of tea?"

"I would love one," Brooke said as she followed Ann into her kitchen. "Can I ask you a question, Ann?" Before waiting for an answer, Brooke continued: "This was not the first time something like this happened with Don, was it?"

"No." Ann whispered as she put the teakettle on the stove. "But it was the last straw."

Brooke took a seat at Ann's kitchen table. "The first instance of 'abuse' happened right after we got engaged," Ann said. She stopped moving. "Sorry. I have trouble using that word. Looking back now, I can say the verbal and psychological abuse started at the very beginning, when we were first dating. I just didn't realize it at the time. It ebbed and flowed through the years until recently. In the last year or two, it has become unbearable, and I knew in my gut that something drastic was about to happen."

Brooke spent the next several hours talking to Ann, gathering background information about the previous abuse and anything specifically directed at the kids. She knew it was much nicer to do this in the comfort of Ann's home, rather than asking her these questions down at the station, where Ann might feel she'd done something to deserve what happened to her.

Brooke looked at the time on the oven and saw it was already 3:50 P.M. "I didn't realize it was getting so late. Thank you so much for your time today, Ann."

"Thank you, Detective. I appreciate having all the allies I can get right now." Ann walked Brooke to the front door.

Once in her car, Brooke debated going back to the office. She was juggling the few other cases she had gotten from Benji. She weighed her need to brush up on them against the idea of ending the day on a positive note, knowing she had supported Ann. She decided the responsible thing to do would be to go back to work—not go home, pour a glass of Merlot, and watch Netflix, which is what she wanted to do. Those activities were definitely on her to-do list for later, though, she decided. Today, last night, yesterday—they had all drained her reserves, and Brooke could hear her bathtub calling her name.

As she drove back to the station, she thought of neutral things like the shows airing on TV that night. As she parked in the staff lot, she promised herself *just an hour to get caught up on things.*

After she walked through the side door that was closest to her office, she found Nick sitting at her desk, in her chair, waiting for her.

"I figured I would wait you out. You had to come back at some point," he said.

"Here I am." Brooke threw her bag on her desk, making a louder noise than she had intended. *Now I wish going home had won out.*

"I see that. Still angry with me?" Nick took his feet down from her desk and sat upright.

"I don't know." Arms crossed, she leaned on the old filing cabinet in the corner, where Benji had stood just yesterday.

"Knew you couldn't stay mad at me." He winked.

"It's not that. I honestly don't know how I feel, which is why I have been ignoring you. Do you remember what you said to me right before you answered your phone last night? While we were on the sidewalk?" Brooke hoped the innuendo he'd poured out was not just a drunken moment. Or maybe she did. *When will this waffling stop?*

Nick took a deep breath. He looked down at his hands, balled up on the desk, and then up and directly into Brooke's blue eyes. "Yes, I remember."

"OK." Brooke sat down in the chair across from her desk and took a deep breath. "Did you mean it?"

Nick folded his arms. "I did."

"You did, or you *do*?"

Nick sighed. He got up, shut the door, and sat back down. "Do you want to have this conversation right now?"

"I don't know." As she said it, she realized she did indeed want to have the conversation, on her terms. She could tell he was apprehensive, but she was determined not to be the one to bring up their deep-rooted feelings first. Brooke was a traditionalist; she wanted to be wooed, fought for. Fair or not, it was the way it was.

Nick ran his fingers through his hair. "OK, well, I *do*. Brooke, I meant what I said and I still mean it. I wasn't thinking when I answered my phone. Call it a knee-jerk reaction—emphasis on *jerk*, I guess. When I turned around and you were gone, I realized what I had just done. And did, I felt like a real jerk." Nick leaned toward her, his hand reaching across the desk, likely hoping she'd grasp it.

She didn't. Instead, Brooke waited for him to continue. She was not going to let him get off the hook this time – if she did, it would perpetuate their weird dance, and it had to stop.

"I'm sorry," he said. She still didn't respond. "Brooke, say something to me, please. Don't just sit there in silence." His eyebrows pinched together, causing them to look like one long line of light hair across his lower forehead.

Brooke realized she was truly finished with going back and forth in this coquettish relationship. Maybe it was the push from Cassie and Jacs that gave her courage, or maybe she was tired of getting hurt, but she wanted the platonic flirting to end, one way or another. "How long do you think we are going to go around in circles before one of us yells 'uncle'?" Her heart rate escalated, knowing an ultimatum might follow. She didn't want to lose Nick, but she also didn't want to play this game forever.

"Honestly, I've been waiting on you," Nick said.

Brooke offered a long, exaggerated blink. When her eyes opened, she asked, "You've what?" *Cassie and Jacs were right.*

He ran his fingers through his hair again—a telltale sign of his anxiety. "Look, I am well aware that you are out of my league." Brooke snorted. Nick ignored it and kept talking. "The last thing I want is to make a move and have you pass. That would destroy us, what we have. Sometimes when I flirt with you, you flirt back. Other times, I think I'm just annoying you." He sighed and looked away, perhaps embarrassed by his honesty.

Brooke's head swam with emotion. Just as she opened her mouth to respond, there was a knock on the door. It was Officer D'Angusto, a fellow patrol officer who was often paired with Nick.

"Hey, Simons, I thought I saw you walk in here. You clocked in yet? They're calling all units to a massive accident right at the Telegraph exit on 95. You in?"

"I'll be right there." Nick rose to leave, never breaking eye contact with Brooke.

As Officer D'Angusto thanked him and walked out, Nick and Brooke stared at each other. "This conversation is far from over," he said as he grabbed her shoulder and squeezed it on his way past her. His face had softened, and it gave Brooke instant butterflies.

"I agree. We really do need to talk," Brooke replied, leaning forward to grab his hand. His fingers closed around hers, providing a warmth that traveled to her toes. She gave him a return squeeze.

"Can I come over tonight? Maybe we can finally finish this conversation… since we probably should have had it four years ago."

Brooke nodded. This was a conversation she wanted to have with him—one that was needed. She was now certain; she wanted them to be more than friends. *It's finally time.* The butterflies morphed into hummingbirds in her belly.

Nick let go of her hand and left. As he turned his back to her, he said, "I'll text you when I'm done at the scene. Love you, Hill."

She watched him go. "Love you, too, Simons."

The words hit her differently than they ever had before.

CHAPTER 10

"Why are they yelling, Brooke? Daddy sounds so mad."

"It's OK, Cassie. Let's cuddle up under the covers. Remember what Mommy always says: we need to be brave."

"But I'm scared..."

"Girls, we have to go. Now!"

The running... the smell of gasoline... "Cassie, stay with me. Hold my hand!"

"Where's Mommy?"

The fire. It's so hot and bright...

———

Brooke woke up shivering, her pajamas were soaked through to her sheets with sweat. It was just a dream, an intense dream. She ran to the bathroom and splashed warm water on her face to avert the chill, then cool water to assuage the nausea.

Crawling back into bed, she checked her phone again. There was still no text from Nick. Between the nightmare and checking her phone almost every hour since 11:00, she'd barely slept. It was now 3:15 A.M. Her stomach rumbled—she'd skipped dinner, choosing to wait for Nick, hoping he'd join her for what she imagined would have been a romantic meal.

As she lay awake, watching the digital clock count down the minutes of sleep she was losing, she wondered if Nick was still stuck at the accident scene. It was too long for a routine clean-up and paperwork—perhaps there was a fatality, or maybe he just hadn't wanted to wake her up. Or maybe he had lost his nerve or changed his mind, and he didn't want to pursue anything past friendship.

"This is not me!" she yelled, finally jumping out of bed at 5:30 and into a hot shower.

Thirty minutes later, with a hot cup of coffee in her hand, she felt rejuvenated and ready to start the day. As an exclamation point on her new, positive energy, she silenced all alerts from Nick. *He should have texted by now*, she decided.

As Brooke arrived at the station and entered her office—now with her third cup of coffee in hand—she saw there was a note taped to the top of her desk. It was an old-fashioned, handwritten one, and she recognized Nick's sloppy penmanship right away:

Hill, I just clocked out. It's just after 3:00 A.M. I don't want to wake you, and I know when you see I didn't text you, you're going to be miffed. I'm hoping this letter will work as a peace offering.

You and I have been close for the better part of six years now, and for those six years, I have looked forward to talking to you every day. Honestly, it's the best part of my day.

What I said the other night slipped out. I was looking at you, and Brooke, you are so beautiful. I just decided to take a chance... and then I effed it all up.

I'm not good with this stuff~you know that. I guess what I am trying to say is I'm ready. Are you?

~Nick

Brooke gripped the letter, reading it two more times, memorizing each word. She switched the alerts on her phone back on. There was already a message from him: *I left you something on your desk.*

She responded immediately: *I just read it… three times actually. And???*

Brooke stared at the phone; she didn't know what to say or even what to think. Nick had always been her friend, one whom she fantasized would someday be more. But now that the opportunity was there, and she wasn't sure what to do. Did she want to pursue a romantic relationship with Nick? Was that a good idea? Suddenly, their friendship meant more to her than she ever realized. *Was it worth risking?*

Just then, her cell phone rang. Ann Reese's name popped up on the screen. Brooke groaned as the reminder of her big, emotional case slapped her like a wet pool noodle.

"Good morning, Ann. Everything OK?"

"Brooke, I think he's watching me." Ann sounded rattled. "I'm hiding in my car in the garage."

Brooke sat down. "What do you mean, you think he's watching you? Did you have the camera passwords changed? Your brother changed the locks, right?"

"Yes, all of that, and the private investigator is coming this morning to sweep the house. But I think there is another way he's watching. Officer Palasco was here last night—I work with his mom, and she suggested he come over and help answer some questions I had about the protective order and the hearing on Friday."

Palasco, Palasco… where had Brooke heard that name before? She typed a text to Nick and Dan Beal, asking if they knew an Officer Palasco.

"OK…" she said, prompting Ann to continue her story.

"Just as he was leaving, I got a text from a number I didn't recognize. It said, 'It's only been two days. How could you bring another man into the house? Way to confuse the kids, Ann.'"

Ann took a breath before continuing. "I was really freaked out, but I was determined not to let him get to me. Then, this morning, Emma was running around before school, trying to help me with the trash cans, and I got another text from a mystery number. This time, it said, 'How can you let a four-year-old run around without a jacket on this cold morning?'... It wasn't even that cold!"

"Was it the same number or different numbers each time?" Brooke asked, trying to restart her computer and take notes.

"Different numbers. And just now, as I was picking up the phone to call you, I got another text. This was from a third number. Brooke, it was just the emoji eyes." Ann's voice was shaking even more.

"Did Don have cameras outside of the house?"

"Only one at the door. My brother took that down, and he put up four outside the house for me, but Don wouldn't know about them."

"What about your neighbors? Does anyone else on the street have outside cameras? Anyone who was close with Don?"

What Brooke didn't say was that she agreed with Ann; Don Reese was probably stalking her, but she couldn't figure out how. With her laptop finally working, she pulled up the addresses of the other six houses in close proximity to Ann's, trying to see if any of the homeowners' names rang a bell.

"Everyone has at least a doorbell camera. It came as a security package when we built the house. We are—or were—pretty close with most of them, especially after the cul-de-sac filled up this past spring. I have a feeling what happened this weekend probably ruined all that." Ann forced a little laugh.

"OK, what time is the private investigator coming?"

"He should be here around ten o'clock, and then I have a noon appointment with the lawyers."

"Right. Here is what we are going to do: I want you to look around at any house that has a view of yours—look for cameras. I'm going to come over at ten and be there when the investigator is there to do his search. Are the kids at school?"

Brooke hoped she was portraying herself as a calm, cool, and collected authority figure. Flashes of her nightmare from last night swam through her mind. She shook her head as Ann continued.

"Yes, I just dropped them off—I did not want them home for any of this. I'm talking to you in my car just in case the house is bugged. I think I've watched too many episodes of *CSI*."

"No, I think you are dead right to… sorry." Brooke internally chastised herself for using the word *dead*. "Go look for the cameras and then hang tight in the house with your alarm on. I'll be there shortly."

Brooke hung up and looked at her messages, still trying to shake off her uneasy feeling. There was one from Beal: *Palasco works at West Springfield, first name Patrick. Think a year behind us at the academy. Solid dude.*

She typed out a message only to Nick: *Hey, the Reese case is imploding, or feels like it is. I need time to process this (you and me). Can we do drinks or dinner tonight?*

Tomorrow works, he replied.

Brooke's chest tightened as disappointment coursed through her.

———

"Tomorrow? Why couldn't he do tonight?" Cassie asked Brooke on FaceTime. Her face was covered with green goo from a face mask, but even that couldn't hide her annoyance.

"No idea." Brooke had asked herself the same question. *What is he doing tonight? Is he going to be with Liv? Did he regret saying what he said?* She propped the phone up on her laptop and tied her hair back into a ponytail. It had already been a long day, and it was only 9:15 A.M. "Maybe he's working tonight. He worked an eleven-hour shift last night. He could just be tired."

Cassie sighed. "You don't honestly believe that, do you?"

"No, I think he is probably going out with his girlfriend, and saying that out loud really sucks." Brooke put her head in her hands.

"Maybe he's breaking up with her since he pretty much proclaimed his love for you?" Cassie said hopefully.

Brooke shrugged and took a big sip of her cold coffee. "Maybe. Anyway, I've got to run—work is piling up. I'll see you on Friday."

"Don't even think about not calling me the minute you talk to him tomorrow!"

"I will, or at least text—I promise." Brooke hung up, still feeling deflated. She was startled to see Benji leaning in the doorway.

"How's Cassie?" he asked.

"How long have you been standing there?"

He smirked. "Long enough." Brooke guessed he had heard way more than she would have wanted.

"We can discuss your love life later. Carol wouldn't want to miss that conversation. I came to check on you and see how the Reese case is going."

Brooke filled Benji in on the latest, including the most recent phone call from Ann. "He must have a camera outside somewhere that she has yet to find," Benji said, as he tried to lean back in the ancient chair across from Brooke's desk. He winced as it groaned underneath him.

"I know, I need new chairs—thanks for leaving these to me, by the way…and that's what I am thinking too—the PI should be able to find it when he sweeps the house." Brooke checked the time and realized it was getting away from her.

Benji knew she needed to get going if she was going to make it to the Reeses' to be there with the PI, so he stood up to take his leave. "I know you need to head out. Keep me posted on how it goes. Who's she using for a PI?"

"Hold on, I have it written down somewhere." Brooke searched the Reese file on her desk. "Chris Hummel. You ever work with him?"

Benji laughed, turned, and shuffled through the doorway. "I have. He's good," he called out as he disappeared from sight.

"Oh no, what? What aren't you telling me?" Brooke yelled back, a sense of dread washing over her.

Benji popped back into view. "Let's just say he's a little eccentric." He winked and was gone again.

CHAPTER 11

Eccentric was an understatement. Private Investigator Chris Hummel looked like Doc Brown from *Back to the Future*, and he carried the gear of someone auditioning for *Ghostbusters*. His baffling white hair and oversized backpack of gear strapped high on his back kept the mood much lighter than expected. "I keep waiting for him to yell, 'Great Scott!'" Ann whispered in Brooke's ear. Brooke laughed—she was stunned that Ann could still crack a joke after the week she had been having.

While PI Hummel was a character, he was also skilled, just as Benji had promised. He looked through Ann's car, inside the house, outside the house, and in every electronic device. His inspection took almost two hours. He found nothing at the Reeses' residence, but he noticed a camera at her neighbor's house pointed directly at hers.

"Not a lot you can do about a camera in someone else's house," he said before leaving. "Hope I never see you on the news, Mrs. Reese."

Ann was taken aback. "What the heck?" she asked Brooke as she closed the door.

"What the heck is right." Brooke was dumbfounded by the PI's nonchalant candor.

"Is he right? Is there really nothing I can do about the neighbor's camera pointed at the house?"

Brooke grimaced. "If it's inside their house, we can't. They have a right to point a camera in any direction, and the way it's angled, they are going to say they are pointing it toward the cul-de-sac for safety reasons." Brooke eyed Ann as she sat down on her couch and put her head in her hands. "It *is*, however, illegal for them to give access to someone who has a protective order against you. The problem is, we don't have any proof that's where Don has his eyes."

"So I just have to deal with it? Well, this sucks."

Brooke's heart went out to Ann, who looked so deflated. "I'm so sorry, Ann. What I can do, if you are comfortable with it, is go door-to-door and let each of your neighbors know you have a protective order against your husband. I may drop a hint or two to certain neighbors that it's illegal to give Don access to a camera trained to watch you."

Tears glistened in Ann's eyes. "Yes, thank you...please."

"OK, not a problem. I'm happy to help."

Ann looked at her watch. "Do you need me to stay around? I have that meeting with the lawyers, and I'm already late." She reached for a tissue.

"No, go. I can handle this. Call me if you need anything."

"Thank you again, Brooke."

Brooke and Ann walked out through the front door together. As Brooke watched Ann drive away, she strolled through the cul-de-sac and let each neighbor know, as promised, that Ann had a protective order against Don. Brooke saved the house with the suspicious camera for last.

When she rang the doorbell, a middle-aged man with a scraggly beard and coffee-colored eyes set close together answered. "Can I help you?" he asked. He looked disheveled, with long, unkempt hair and clothes two sizes too big for him.

"I'm not sure if you are aware, but there was an incident at one of your neighbors' houses—the Reeses—this past weekend. Mr. Reese is no longer living at the residence, and Mrs. Reese has a protective order against him." Brooke could tell by the look on this particular neighbor's face that he was not a fan of cops. He stared at her blankly, as if she was the teacher speaking in the *Peanuts* movies, and he wasn't going to listen.

Brooke continued anyway. "I wanted to make sure you were aware, Mr...." Still nothing. "Sir, what is your name?" she asked. She wanted to cross her arms, but she kept them at her sides in case she needed to reach for her gun.

"You're a cop. Don't you know my name?" His self-righteous smirk aggravated her, and she took a breath to calm herself.

Great, Brooke thought. *He* is *one of those.* "Sir, I can go back to my cruiser and look up your name, or you could save me a walk and just tell me. If I have to walk, I might stumble over something you don't want me to..." It was a veiled threat she knew she wouldn't be able to keep.

"Murray," he spat out.

Brooke lost her patience. "Mr. Murray, you have a camera pointed directly at Mrs. Reese's property." No sense in delaying the direct course anymore.

He laughed. "It's not pointed *at* her house. It's pointed at the cul-de-sac, where the kids play."

"Right, it also gives direct views of her driveway and front door. I want to make sure you are aware, Mr. Murray, that surveillance of any kind by Mr. Reese is illegal. And so is helping him." Brooke knew she had to be careful with her word choices; she could not allege he was giving Don Reese access to his camera, even though she was willing to bet he was.

"Detective Hill, what exactly are you accusing me of?" Mr. Murray asked.

"Nothing. I just want to make sure you are aware. Have a good day, Mr. Murray."

With that, she turned and heard the door close behind her.

As Brooke walked back to her cruiser, she pulled out her cell phone and called the station. "Hey, June, it's Detective Hill. I want to request a patrol for Sherwood Way in Harbor Meadows for the next forty-eight hours. Specifically, number 1511. Thanks."

CHAPTER 12

Brooke lived fifteen minutes south of the station in an old neighborhood with ranch-style houses on more land than what developers now allotted for homeowners in newer subdivisions. Brooke's gray-brick home with black shutters sat on a full acre and had been updated several times since the 1975 original build date. Brooke bought it two years ago, and every weekend morning, she shuffled across the engineered hardwood flooring in her fuzzy socks and sat in the sunlight of her bright white kitchen. The previous owners had chosen well during the redecorating.

After pulling into her carport and entering her kitchen through the mudroom, Brooke gave herself a generous pour of red wine. She still felt annoyed after her interaction with Mr. Murray, but she tried to stay positive. She knew Ann's scraggly neighbor had to be the one giving camera access to Don Reese. She just wasn't sure how the technology worked, or why he'd do that for Don. *Maybe he's just an ornery kinda guy. Or maybe he hates women...*

She was still pondering this as she changed clothes and then washed her face. As soon as she patted her cheeks dry, she heard three knocks on her front door.

She was surprised to see Nick standing on her porch. "Hi," she managed to get out.

Nick had changed out of his police uniform and into what he called his "other" uniform: a black T-shirt and Wrangler jeans. "Hi. Can I come in?"

"Yeah, of course." Brooke let him in and quickly checked herself in the mirror hanging in the foyer. She had thrown on an old George Mason college sweatshirt and black leggings, and her hair was in a sloppy ponytail. As she glanced at her reflection, she suddenly regretted washing her make-up off. *Not my best*, she thought.

"I thought we were on for tomorrow? Did I miss a text?" Brooke asked.

"No. I had to see you now." Nick walked into the family room and turned toward her.

"OK. I have to be honest… I don't know that I have my thoughts together enough to have the conversation we need to have." Brooke felt like she was holding it together pretty well, but then Nick smirked. "What's with the smirk?"

"I was thinking of something really inappropriate to say, like, 'Who said anything about talking?' But I thought that was probably the wrong thing to say at this moment. I realize we really do need to have a grown-up conversation."

They both laughed, and it broke the tension. He crossed the room and touched her face. "But what if I was serious, Hill? What if I didn't want to just talk? At least until later?"

"Nick—" Brooke said as a flash of heat hit her chest.

He stopped her sentence with a kiss, placed softly on the lips—more of a brush than making full impact, and Brooke felt a tingling sensation course through her body.

This kiss was different from the first one years ago. That had been playful, flirty. This kiss had intent and meaning behind it, a controlled passion.

Nick kissed her again when Brooke didn't push him away. This time, it was stronger, deeper.

"Nick…" Brooke managed to get his name out after the second kiss.

"Yes?" he purred in her ear.

"This is going to change everything."

"That's what I'm hoping." He placed his hands on either side of Brooke's face and looked into her blue eyes.

———

The next thing Brooke knew, she was lying next to Nick, naked, at the foot of her bed. She spied her leggings and sweatshirt on the floor near the door of the bedroom and her black lace panties and bra lay next to the bed, just below her. The sun was setting through the window, casting an orange glow on her pale blue walls.

"That was…" Nick started.

When he didn't finish, Brooke did. "Yeah, it was." She smiled at the man with his legs wrapped around hers.

Nick's phone buzzed from his pants pocket. His Wranglers had landed at the head of the bed, covering her pillow. He grabbed his phone and glanced at the screen. Brooke couldn't help looking at his phone too. Liv was calling. Brooke rolled over as Nick silenced the phone.

"We should get up," she said, sitting up and reaching for a blanket so she could make it to her clothes. Where a few minutes ago, she was confident and comfortable, now, she suddenly felt very, very exposed.

"Brooke, wait." Nick ran his fingers through his blond hair. Brooke turned her head to look at him over her shoulder. His eyes seemed sincere. "I don't know how to navigate this."

"Neither do I."

"Then maybe, for now, we lie back down, and we don't worry about how to." He winked.

Brooke stared straight ahead for a few seconds, then relented. Soon, they were tangled up together once again.

Before they could get far, Brooke's phone buzzed from the bedside table where she'd left it charging before Nick ever arrived.

"Hang on, let me put it on silent," she said, and Nick did not let her go easily. As Brooke reached for her phone, though, she saw the caller's name: *Ann Reese*. She jumped up and answered the call immediately, turning on her bedside lamp. "Ann? Are you OK?"

The voice on the phone was not Ann's. "Hey, Detective Hill, this is Officer Patrick Palasco. Ann is next to me—we just called the non-emergency number for the station, and they are sending someone out. Ann thought we should call you as well. Hang on, I'll put her on."

"Brooke?" Ann was hard to understand. Sniffling took up most of her communication.

"Ann, what's going on? What happened?" Now Nick was sitting up next to Brooke.

"He's watching me! I got another text from a number I didn't recognize. Pat had come over again because I wanted to ask him what he thought about the camera and the PI's work."

She calls him Pat? Brooke refocused on what Ann was saying.

"It's his day off, so he didn't have his cruiser. I had him pull into the garage, and within thirty seconds of him walking in my door, I got the text. It said, 'I can't believe you let him park in the garage.'" Ann began sobbing.

"Oh no, Ann. I'm so sorry." Nick rubbed Brooke's back as she consoled the woman on the other end of the line.

"Pat directed me to tell him to stop stalking me—to use those exact words—so I did. Then I got another message about how stupid

I am and what an awful mother I am. I blocked the number, and Pat called the non-emergency number for me. Now we're waiting for another officer to get here." Brooke heard something that sounded like a cross between a sigh and a loud sob.

"Where are the kids?" Brooke turned to look at Nick, and he gave her a knowing smile.

"I sent them to the next-door neighbors' house. I didn't want them to be here when the police came."

"Ann, I am about twenty minutes away from you right now—I'll be there shortly. Tell the officer who responds that I'm on my way."

Brooke hung up and raced around the room, grabbing her clothes strewn about the floor. She texted Beal and asked him to meet her at the Reeses' house. Then she turned to Nick, who was still sitting up in bed, shirtless and wrapped in her sheets, his hair a mess.

"Hey," she said with a smile.

He smiled back. "Go. Not like I don't get it."

"I'm so sorry."

"I can think of a few ways you can make it up to me."

She kissed him passionately with her hand behind his head, pulling him closer to her. "To be continued."

As she walked out of the bedroom, she looked down at her phone. Beal had just responded. *Roger that, boss. Just heard the call come in. Reed's almost there. I'm right behind him.*

Brooke grabbed her keys and headed out. As she closed the side door leading to her carport, she could have sworn she heard Nick say, "Hey, babe," but her adrenaline was raging at such a high level, his words wouldn't register until later.

CHAPTER 13

As Brooke pulled up to the Reeses' residence, she saw two squad cars, both without their lights on. *Good call*, thought Brooke, *no need to draw the kids' attention.*

Beal opened the front door when Brooke knocked. "Detective Hill," he said.

"Officer Beal." Brooke looked past him and saw Officer Reed, who looked young enough to have just stepped off a high school football field. His broad shoulders stretched his uniform to seem as if he'd just ironed it. "Officer Reed."

"Detective," Officer Reed said. "Congratulations, by the way."

"Thanks." She half-smiled and looked past him to the stairs. Sitting on the third step was Ann, her face in her hands. Seated next to her was the man Brooke assumed was Officer Palasco. He looked kind, especially his eyes, and she could see why Ann would seek comfort from him. The second he undraped his arm from around Ann's shoulders, Beal nudged her. She must have been staring.

Officer Palasco stood up. "Detective Hill, I'm Officer Patrick Palasco. It's nice to meet you. I had the pleasure of working with Detective Noble from time to time."

They shook hands. "Nice to meet you, and thank you for calling me." Brooke turned her attention to Ann. "Ann, how are you holding up?"

Ann's eyes were puffy and red from crying. "I've been better."

Brooke squeezed her arm. "What do we know?" she asked the room. As she looked around, she smelled the leftover odors of an Italian-inspired dinner. Her stomach threatened to growl—she'd never eaten. Her cheeks flushed pink with the secret of what she had been doing for the past few hours. She bit her lip, waiting for an answer from one of the officers surrounding her.

Officer Reed spoke up: "I was first at the scene. Mrs. Reese showed me a string of text messages she received from numbers she doesn't recognize. Then Officer Beal arrived, and we showed him the messages. Mrs. Reese recounted the events involving Officer Palasco that led up to the messages, and she also informed us about the PI's sweep and the neighbor's camera."

"I went door-to-door earlier today—" Brooke looked at her watch to make sure it was still the same day; she had been awake for such a long time at this point. "I spoke with Mr. Murray across the way—he has a camera pointed directly at the driveway here. I informed him that giving access to Mr. Reese is a violation of the protective order and is illegal."

"Ha!" Ann scoffed. "How'd he take that?"

"Well, I don't think he is going to be inviting me over for coffee anytime soon," Brooke said with a smirk.

"He's always been crazy; I just didn't think he was crazy enough to give Don camera footage." Ann put her head in her hands again.

"Well, we don't have proof," Brooke reminded her.

"Ann, do you know where your husband is?" Beal asked.

"No. Last I heard, he was staying with a family friend in Annapolis. I'm not sure if that was just overnight or if he's there 'til he finds another place."

Beal, Reed, Palasco, and Brooke looked at one another. No one wanted to tell this poor woman what they were all thinking: there was no possible way to trace these messages back to her husband, and there was also no legal way to confront the neighbor again, at least not yet.

"Mrs. Reese, we can file a police report stating what you have just told us," Officer Reed said, "but—"

Ann cut him off. "There's nothing you can do." She had tears in her eyes.

Beal cleared his throat. "Mrs. Reese, we can't prove it's him texting you, and we can't prove he has access to the neighbor's camera. We would need a warrant to go into Mr. Murray's house, and no judge is going to give us that on this little information. If we file a report, it will be brought up when you go to court for the incident this past weekend, which everyone in this room will be at."

Ann was incredulous. "I don't believe this! This man is going to make my life a nightmare, and there is really nothing I can do about it besides grin and bear it?"

Brooke knelt down next to the woman as her heart strained with the memories of her own story. "Ann, we will file the report, and in the morning, I will call a Commonwealth attorney I know. I'll see if I can poke around and find out who will have the case, and then I'll see if I can speak to them and give them some background information. This is your best bet at the moment."

"Fine." Ann didn't look up but turned in Officer Palasco's direction. "Will you stay on the couch?" Everyone in the room tried not to notice the unusual—and intimate—request.

Palasco cleared his throat. "Yes, of course."

Brooke stood up. "Officer Palasco, you need to let your lieutenant know about this case, if you haven't already. Your name will be in the police report that Officer Reed will be writing up."

"I called him already. Thanks." Brooke couldn't tell exactly what was going on between Ann Reese and Officer Palasco, but it was defi-

nitely something. She wondered if this was what people thought—
what they felt—when she and Nick were in the same room.

"OK, Officer Reed, why don't you head back to the station
to type up your report?" she said. "Officer Beal and I will take a
walk around the neighborhood for a bit to look around and let
our presence be known. I already put the order in to have more
patrols in the area. I'll also radio dispatch to make sure the message got through."

"Thank you," Ann mouthed to Brooke.

"Are the kids still next door?" Brooke asked, looking around.

"Yes, I need to go get them."

Brooke pointed to the back door. "Bring them in through the
back so they don't see the cruisers while Officer Beal and I do our
walkabout. And Ann, turn on the alarm as soon as you get everyone
safely inside."

Ann nodded, and the three of them left Ann with Officer Palasco.

Outside, Beal looked at Brooke. "Think they are banging?"

Brooke eyed him and nudged him with her elbow. She whispered,
"I'm just wondering for how long... but you didn't hear that from
me." Her words were light-hearted, but her tone was serious. *I'm a
detective now. I should be the professional one.*

As the two toured the neighborhood, Brooke pointed to the Murrays' house across the cul-de-sac. There was a large red and white "no
soliciting" sign on the door, and on a street where everyone had their
outdoor lights on, the Murrays' house was pitch black but for the
glow of a light in an upper room, likely a bedroom.

Beal nodded in the direction Brooke was pointing. "They
seem friendly."

"Very charming. I only had the pleasure of meeting Mr. Murray."

"Sweep you off your feet, did he?"

They spent the next twenty minutes circling the cul-de-sac and talking about Beal's three beautiful girls and his wife's desire to try for a boy.

When they parted, Beal said he was going to take over the patrol route for the Reese residence, and Brooke radioed into the station to make sure the request for extra police presence on Sherwood Way had gone through. It had, and she was assured more squad cars would be circling the Reese house for the next forty-eight hours. This gave Brooke some comfort, and she hoped it would for Ann as well.

———————

By the time Brooke returned to her house, it was inching past midnight, and she felt her eyes growing heavier with each passing minute. Too exhausted to shower, she crept back into her bed fully clothed. She was surprised to find a naked Nick Simons lying next to her, waiting.

"You're still here?" Brooke rolled toward him. "I didn't even notice your car."

"I parked down the street. And I told you: you were going to make it up to me."

He kissed her, and suddenly, Brooke didn't feel so tired after all.

CHAPTER 14

"**Y**ou had sex?" Jacs yelled.

It was way too early for Brooke to be heading into work—and too early for this conversation. She regretted answering the phone while driving. "How in the world did you get that with just me saying hello? What are you doing up this early, anyway?"

"Spin class. Don't change the subject. Spill."

Brooke rolled her eyes but then went on to tell her best friend every detail.

She could hear Jacs honk her car's horn. "Move out of the effing way! Sorry—no one can drive this morning. So what, was he still there this morning?"

"Yes, I woke up with Nick Simons in my bed." Fighting every urge to maintain some integrity, Brooke let out a squeal.

"Wow!"

"I know."

"I'm impressed. I really didn't think you had it in you. Figured we'd be sharing a bottle of tequila on Nick's wedding day to drown your sorrows after watching him kiss the bride." She honked her horn again and let out a few more choice words.

Brooke pulled into the station. "Thanks for the support." She was smiling, though.

"So, you know you still have to have the talk about where things stand and what is going on, right?"

Brooke's smile faded. "Yeah, I know. We said something in passing about that as I was leaving." It had been more Brooke saying they should probably still have that conversation, and Nick once again convincing her that talking was overrated. The smile returned.

"Hello?" Jacs yelled into the phone.

"Yeah, I'm here... sorry." Brooke snapped out of it, shaking her head.

"I was saying I'll meet you at Freddie's tonight after work. I want more details."

"I just told you everything!... But I'll see you there."

"Tequila shots on me tonight, you hussy!"

Brooke looked in her rearview mirror, relieved that she had left Nick sleeping in her bed and didn't have to face him right now in front of everyone else.

She knew they needed to have "the talk" and she was nervous, though she couldn't figure out why. He clearly had feelings for her, and she for him. It was time to see where things would go, but what if he just wanted things to stay casual?

She didn't think she could be OK with that. She remembered him basically telling her he wanted things to go to the next level before all this happened, but Brooke couldn't ignore the red warning flag flapping deep in her gut. Intuition was usually her strength—she wished she could just ignore it and go all in with Nick Simons.

After parking and walking halfway to her office, she realized she had left her coffee in the car. *Get your head on right, Hill.* While retrieving it, she found Benji in the parking lot. "You know," Brooke said, "I see you at the station more now than when you actually worked here."

"Well, I came for two reasons. The first is I ran into Beal just now at CVS, and he told me what happened last night. The second is Cassie called Carol, and I was given implicit instructions to make sure you were there on Sunday. She apparently spoke to Talia, who is not thrilled with you. Apparently, you haven't called her back."

"Crap." Brooke pulled out her phone. "I just set a reminder to call Aunt T back. And I will be there on Sunday, I promise."

"Great. That at least gets Carol off my back." Benji chuckled. "Let's head to my office and you can fill me in on last night." He started walking, but Brooke didn't follow. She took a sip of her coffee and leaned against her car, smiling at him.

He cleared his throat and corrected himself. "*Your* office."

"Thanks, Benji," she said as she walked past him.

Cramming into the office, they both sat down. It still smelled like commercial disinfectant, and Brooke made a mental note to buy an air purifier. Once seated, she filled Benji in on the text messages and the cameras. "I know he's watching her, and I know that jerk neighbor of hers has given him access to it. I just can't prove it."

"I'm sure you're right, or he had a camera placed somewhere else that is motion-censored. Did Hummel check outside too?"

"He did, and by the way, eccentric doesn't even begin to describe your PI friend," Brooke said with a laugh.

"I told you! But he is good. What's your game plan now?"

"I told Mrs. Reese I would call one of the Commonwealth attorneys I know and see if I can dig around as to who the case has been assigned to, or at least give the attorney some background information on what has transpired. Figured it was our best shot. Don Reese's attorney is Greg Levine."

Benji whistled as he crossed his large legs. "He must have some money to blow. I do not miss having to deal with Levine."

"Well, according to him, you are best friends. Even called to tell me so."

Benji winced. "Yeah, that's not the word I would use for us." He stood up. "All right, I'm off. I promised Carol I would be right back so we could go to breakfast. Keep me posted, and remember to call Talia back."

"I will. I told you I set a reminder on my phone, see? It's right here." As Brooke pulled out her phone, she saw she had a text from Nick. She blushed instantly.

"Oh, yeah, reminder. OK, well, you get back to your phone and tell Simons I said hi." Benji chuckled.

After Benji left, Brooke smiled and looked at her message. It was a shirtless picture of Nick, still in her bed: *Miss you in here with me.*

Brooke wrote back: *You should stay.*

Can't. I've just been called in for an extra shift. Maybe we check and see how sturdy that desk of yours really is later today.

Brooke hid the screen against her chest. *Yup, I'm in trouble.* Brooke smiled to herself. She knew she had to put her phone down or she would never get any work done. But there was one more thing she needed it for; she searched for the phone number for Brian Keenan, the Commonwealth attorney she knew. He and Jacs had dated back when they were all in college, but nothing had come of it.

Brian picked up after several rings. "Hi, Brian, this is Detective Brooke Hill." Brooke put a hand on her forehead; she knew she did not need to be that formal with Brian.

"Detective now? Good job, Brookie," he said with a laugh. Brooke remembered Brian back in college. He'd been classically handsome—tall with dark, walnut-colored hair cut into a short crew style. She couldn't help but wonder if he still had the muscles Jacs used to lust over. She pictured him leaning back in some swanky office chair, talking to her.

"To what do I owe the pleasure of speaking to *Detective* Hill after all these years?" Brian continued to emphasize her title. She didn't mind.

"It has been a while, hasn't it? Sorry. Actually, I'm hoping you can help me. Any chance I can ask an old college friend for a favor? I'm hoping you can tell me who has been assigned to the Don Reese case. The hearing is tomorrow morning." Brooke tried to sound casual, though she noted the burn of desperation coursing through her veins, hoping she could do something—anything—to help Ann.

"That would be me. I'm reviewing it now, in fact." Brian said.

"Oh, good!" Brooke said a little too enthusiastically. She took a breath and remembered her new lot in life. "I mean, I've been working this case for a bit, and I wanted to give the attorney assigned to it some background information that could be useful. Just happy to hear that it's a friendly."

He laughed. "Unlike some of the trolls we have here?"

"No, that's not what I meant… at least, I don't think that's what I meant." Brooke tried for humor; it worked.

"I'm teasing too. I'm ready when you are."

Brooke filled him in on the past unreported abuse, the current CPS investigation, the neighbor's camera across the street, and the text messages.

"I see there was a police report filed just last night?" Brian asked.

"Yes, I can email it over to you."

"That's fine. I can have a clerk run down and grab it."

"Can I ask what you are thinking about this case, after everything I've just said?"

She heard him laugh under his breath. "You can ask, but I'm not prepared to tell you yet. Look, he's a first offender with a really good lawyer. You and I know he will most likely be offered a first offender disposition, and the wife will be issued a permanent protective order."

Brooke sighed. "Yeah, that's what I figured."

"If I could do more, I would. Listen, I've got to run. It was great to talk to you, even if it was just work stuff. I'd love to grab a drink sometime." Brian said.

"That would be great—we absolutely should. Oh! Hey, Jacs and I are going to Freddie's after work tonight. You should join us." As the words left her mouth, Brooke hoped this would be a good surprise for Jacs.

"You guys still go to Freddie's? Yeah, I'll see if I can break free early. What's your cell?"

After exchanging numbers, they hung up. Despite ending the call on a positive note, Brooke felt deflated, knowing Don Reese was probably going to get away with everything.

CHAPTER 15

Brooke looked at the tequila shot Jacs offered her. "Have you lost your mind? I have to be in court at ten o'clock tomorrow for my first big case. I am not taking that." The air in Freddy's smelled like peanuts and spilled beer, and the bar in the middle of the room was packed, customers standing shoulder to shoulder. The two women were at the far end on the backside of the bar, saving a stool with their jackets in the event a third person showed up to crash their party.

"Fine, more for me." Jacs licked the salt off her hand.

"I'll drink the other one if this seat isn't taken." Brian Keenan's appearance caught them both by surprise.

"Oh, my—Brian!" Jacs jumped off the red linoleum barstool and hugged him. "What are you doing here?" Brooke sighed with relief, grateful for Jacs' reaction to seeing her former flame.

"I was talking to Brooke today—oh wait, I'm sorry, *Detective* Brooke Hill," he said with a wink. "She said you guys still come here. I live right down the street, so thought I'd stop by."

"Hi, Brian," Brooke said as she hugged him. As she did, she caught a whiff of geranium flower, lemon, and cedarwood—it was intoxicating. He wore dark tan chinos with a white button-down shirt, no socks, and brown leather shoes—he looked even more handsome than she remembered. She especially noted the small scar he sported on his forehead near his dark hairline—it gave him more of a rugged look than she remembered, offsetting his clean, pretty-boy face.

As the three of them caught up, Brooke checked her phone. She had one message from Nick: *Hey! I'm knocking off for the night. I'm not making it to Freddie's. Thinking about you, Hill.* Despite herself, Brooke was disappointed. She put her phone back in her pocket and rejoined the conversation.

"Brooke and I are actually going to be spending some time together tomorrow in court," Brian said, nudging her arm.

Jacs stole a side glance at Brooke. They were both thinking the same thing: *is Brian Keenan flirting right now?*

"Yeah, about that," Brooke said. "I really don't think you should offer the first offender disposition. This guy is stalking his wife right now, and I believe he is capable of more. He's dangerous."

Brian put up his hand. "I'm not talking shop right now. We will have plenty of time to discuss this tomorrow in court. I came to catch up with my two college friends."

Jacs yelled, "Here, here!" and clinked glasses with Brian.

Brooke sighed but nodded. After ten minutes of small talk, she stood up from the bar and asked Jacs to get her tab. Making her way to the bathroom, she typed a message to Nick: *Understandable. The tequila shots miss you.*

When Brooke returned a few minutes later, Brian was gone. "Where did he go?" she asked Jacs, who was still seated, belly up to the drink table, scrolling on her phone.

A smile spread across Jacs' face. "He took a phone call outside."

"What? Why are you looking at me like that?" Brooke finished the last sip of her drink.

"*Our* college friend Brian did not come to see both of us, Brooke. He came to see you."

"What makes you say that? We haven't seen each other in ages."

"Oh, no reason. But as soon as you got up, he asked if you were seeing someone." Jacs took a swig of her drink and eyed Brooke teasingly.

"What did you say?" Brooke's heart fluttered.

"I said you aren't seeing anyone and told him he should go for it." Jacs winked.

Brooke stared at her blankly. "Did you really?" Mixed feelings erupted in her chest.

"Yes, I did, and you *aren't* seeing anyone! You slept with a friend last night who you've had a crush on. But Brian is hot... and a nice guy, at least from what I remember. You have nothing to lose, not until you and Nick talk. And don't even try to use me as an excuse—that was a million years ago and meant nothing to either of us." Jacs crossed her arms in a show of force.

Leave it to Jacs to be brutally honest—Brooke wasn't sure if she should be angry or happy. After all, Brian smelled so good... and looked so good...

Jacs shrugged. "Don't be mad. You know I'm right."

"I'm not sure how I feel."

"Well, you can decide later—he's coming back." Jacs gestured to Brian, who was crossing the restaurant and bar, heading straight toward them.

"Sorry about that. Looks like I am going to have to take off. I have to get some files off to my boss. Jacs, it was so good to see you." Brian side-hugged her. "Let's not wait another three years before doing this."

His warm smile melted Brooke's resolve not to get tangled up in anything.

Jacs smiled. "Agreed. You look great, by the way."

"You too." He turned to Brooke. "Brooke, can you walk with me? I want to talk to you about tomorrow."

"Sure." Brooke got up from her barstool, kissed Jacs on the cheek, and followed Brian out. As they strode toward the door, she turned to look over her shoulder to see Jacs smiling after them. Jacs winked, and Brooke shook her head in mock defeat.

Cooler air hit Brooke when she stepped outside. A storm had passed overhead while they were inside, and the chilly air was a reminder that fall was quickly approaching. The sidewalk in front of Freddie's was wet and deserted; it was just the two of them. Brian turned to face her. "I didn't ask you to come out here so we can talk about the case."

"OK." Brooke looked at him, feigning confusion. On the inside, her heart pounded against her rib cage. She looked into Brian's hazel eyes and something in her stirred.

He gazed back into her face. "I'm just going to say it. I've always had a crush on you, even back in college. Don't tell Jacs that part." Brian chuckled, and Brooke half-smiled. "I'd love to take you out sometime."

He is so handsome, Brooke thought. *Maybe I should just go for it.* But then she thought of Nick. She needed to talk to him first; she felt like she owed him that.

"I would love to…" Brooke started.

Brian winced. "There is a 'but' in there somewhere."

Brooke chose honesty and hoped she wouldn't regret it. "There is. I need to figure out what is going on with a very good friend of mine before I date someone else."

Brian seemed to understand. He nodded and said, "I get it. Look, if things fall through, you know how to reach me. Offer stands until Zendaya comes knocking on my door." His comment broke the tension, and they hugged before he turned and walked toward his car.

Brooke looked at her watch. *Screw it,* she thought. *I'm calling him. He's going to have to wake up for this.* She dialed Nick's number and listened to the phone ring.

"Hello?"

It was a woman's voice. Brooke looked at the phone to make sure she had dialed the correct number. She had, and she quickly hung up. The post-storm wind did nothing to cool the heat creeping into her face. And with the surprise on the other end of the phone, air struggled to exit her lungs.

It took a second to get herself together, but when she looked down the street and saw Brian walking away, she called after him. "Hey, Brian, wait up!"

He stopped and turned. When he saw Brooke running after him, he closed the gap.

When she reached him, she was out of breath. "You know... what? Forget... what I said. Yes, let's grab drinks... or dinner... or whatever... soon." Her words came as gasps.

"You sure?"

She nodded and smiled. "Yes, absolutely."

"OK, cool." His magnetic grin erased any outstanding doubt. "Then it's a date. I'll text you later." He kissed her on the cheek. She watched him walk away—even a pending date with a handsome guy like Brian couldn't take away the heartache and betrayal she felt.

CHAPTER 16

I t was early Friday morning, and Brooke was much more dressed up than usual. She had her gray court dress on with black heels. Her dark hair flowed past her shoulders in soft curls. She knew she looked good and knew Brian would appreciate it, but part of her was hoping she would run into Nick.

She did not have to wait long. As she walked into the station, she saw him standing next to June at the dispatch desk. He raised an eyebrow at her, but she continued walking past with barely an acknowledgment. As soon as she sat in her chair, there was a knock at her office door.

"Can I come in?" He looked sheepish.

"Sure." Brooke didn't bother to look up from her computer.

He took a step across the small office toward her. "I know you're mad. Can you give me a minute to explain?"

Brooke looked up. Nick was in uniform and had dark circles under his eyes. "Why would I be mad? Look, we had fun the other night, but it's not like I was under the impression that I was your girl-friend all of a sudden." She couldn't hide the bitter tone in her voice, and she bit her lip to stop her words.

"Brooke..." Nick's eyes were pleading with her to soften her heart.

"Yes, Nick?" She matched his gaze. She wasn't going to back down.

"Liv came over last night, and I broke it off with her. She answered my phone when I went to use the bathroom and didn't tell me until about an hour later, when she was leaving. Trust me—I was furious too."

Brooke slammed down the file that was in her hand. "You actually expect me to believe that?" As much as she tried to wrangle her emotions, she couldn't. The hurt she had felt all night long flew out of her mouth and all over Nick.

"Yes, I expect you to believe me… because it's the truth," he whispered.

"OK."

"OK? So we're good?" Nick looked hopeful, his eyes wide.

"Yep, all good." Brooke was desperate to look anywhere but into his eyes.

"Brooke, come on. Do you really think I'm lying about this? Do you really think I am going to screw up the one shot I have with you?" He ran his fingers through his hair, giving Brooke flashbacks of their time together in bed.

"I don't know. What I do know is I need to grab this file and head to court." Brooke took the file off her desk and tried to move past him and through the doorway.

He grabbed her arm. They were eye to eye now. "Please talk to me."

"I don't want to right now. I need to think. Honestly, I'm hurt, Nick. And I don't know if I believe you."

He took her head in his hands and kissed her. Brooke glanced toward the open door.

He turned her head back to him. "I get it. I do. But you know me, and I would never do anything to screw this up."

Brooke looked down at the floor as Nick released his hands. "I have to go, Nick."

"Will you call me later?"

"I will." And with that, she left.

The drive to the courthouse gave Brooke time to push any thoughts of Nick out of her head. She needed to be on her A-game for her first court appearance in her new role. Ann needed her, and if she was being honest, Brooke needed Ann to be OK, too.

In the waiting area, she spotted Don Reese right away. He was seated next to Greg Levine, and both men were wearing what appeared to be expertly-tailored suits—Mr. Reese's a navy blue and his attorney's a charcoal gray. Brooke tried to walk past them without being noticed, but Greg spotted her, standing up and make a beeline for her.

"Brooke! Good to see you," he said, extending his hand.

"Hi, Greg." Brooke tried her best not to show her disgust and used his first name since he neglected to respect her by using hers. She didn't shake his hand.

"I'd be a lot better if I would have known Ann Reese filed a police report against my client. I thought you would've given me a heads up on that?" Greg tilted his head to one side, and his overly gelled hair didn't move.

"What on earth gave you that impression? I told you I don't comment on ongoing investigations." She was determined not to let him intimidate her this time.

Greg took a step closer. "Interesting. Perhaps we won't be having the same professional relationship I shared with your predecessor."

Brooke smirked. "Perhaps not is right. Now, please excuse me." Brooke stepped around him and walked away. *At least this second face-to-face interaction went better than the first*, she thought. Still, she burned hot on the inside and hated that the weasel was still trying to make her feel inferior.

As she walked down the corridor, she spotted Ann. She was huddled with an older man and woman, whom Brooke assumed were her parents. They all wore their Sunday best, even though it was a Friday. She also spotted Officer Palasco standing close by in full uniform. He could not keep his eyes off of Ann. *Interesting,* Brooke thought.

Beal was standing to the other side of the corridor, dressed very nicely in a dark blue suit with a meticulously ironed, open-collared shirt and no tie. After nodding at Ann and mouthing a hello, Brooke approached him, seeking an ally. "You clean up well, Beal, despite the man-bun," she said.

"I think my man-bun makes the outfit, honestly," he replied, faux-dusting his shoulders with his hand. "They said they would call us into the conference room shortly. Any ideas who the Commonwealth attorney is for this case?"

"Actually, yes. I did a little digging, and it's Brian Keenan."

"Oh, right. I've dealt with him before. Not a bad guy."

Brooke looked around for Brian. "Yeah, we went to college together. I called him yesterday."

"Did he tell you how he was leaning?"

Brooke looked back at Beal. "No, but he mentioned the first offender disposition. I'm afraid that despite everything, that is where this is headed." Brooke still hoped she was wrong.

"I figured; there just isn't enough to go on with the stalking, and this is his first offense." Beal gave Brooke an apologetic look.

"Not your fault," she said.

Just then, a conference door opened to the right of them and Brian Keenan walked out. Brooke tried not to stare at him in his black suit, the color accentuating his greenish-brown eyes and matching his dark brown hair. With the pair of glasses he wore today, he could have passed for Clark Kent's brother. *And those narrow hips…* Brooke blushed. Brian spotted her and gave her a smile, then called them into the conference room. *Let's hope you're the superhero you seem to be...*

Brooke walked in alongside Ann, giving the woman's arm a squeeze. "How are you holding up?" she asked.

Ann sighed. "I have never wanted to have a drink more than I do right now."

Brooke laughed, appreciative of Ann's humor and candid answer. "I understand that." She turned around and introduced herself to Ann's attorney, Bob Woodson. Turning back to Ann, she added, "You picked a good criminal attorney, Ann, but you know you did not need to bring counsel today, right?" Bob gave Brooke a wink and sat down.

"I know. Mr. Woodson wanted to come along so he could be familiar with the case for when we have to get the extension for the protective order."

Once they'd all filed into the small conference room, the space felt cramped, especially once Brian closed the twelve-foot tall, metal-re-inforced door, and the air inside suddenly smelled stale. As everyone sat down around the conference table, all eyes trained on Brian at the head of the long oval.

He cleared his throat and began the introductions. Afterward he said, "Mrs. Reese, I've read over the details of the events of this past weekend. This is your husband's first offense, though I understand you have described a history of domestic violence. This is the first time the police and the Commonwealth have been involved, however, and he has no other priors, so the Commonwealth is going to offer him the first offender disposition."

Brooke inwardly groaned and outwardly sighed—this was what she had been afraid of. She made eye contact with Beal, who frowned slightly.

Brian continued, "What that entails is this: Mr. Reese has to stay on parole for two years. Once he has done that, this will be expunged from his record—as long as there are no further arrests or any legal run-ins regarding this matter. We will give you a permanent protective order, which is good for two years. In the event you want to extend this order, you will need to petition the court before the two-year period is up. Do you have any questions?"

How could anyone not *have any questions?* Brooke thought. Brian had talked so fast, there was no way Ann *couldn't* be confused. Brooke looked around the conference table before her eyes fell on Ann. She could not discern what the woman was thinking; the look spreading across Ann's face could mean so many things.

Finally, Ann spoke: "Hang on. So what you're telling me is that he walks *free?*" Ann asked. Her voice was steady, but there was more than a hint of anger behind it.

"Well, not *free*, per se," Brian said. "He's on parole. This is good; you have the protective order, and if he isn't in jail, he can pay the child support the State will require." He clasped his hands in front of him on the table. His eyes were kind, but Brooke could tell that Ann apparently didn't feel the same way about his words.

"This is utter bull—" Ann spit out. She was stopped mid-sentence by her dad's hand on her shoulder.

Every head turned toward her. Shock slid through Brooke at the hostility of Ann's response, understandable as it was.

Ann's mother put her hand on her daughter's other shoulder and whispered in her ear. Ann nodded and then continued: "That man threatened my life... *and* my children's lives, not to mention that he continues to harass me. And he walks away with a slap on the wrist? My only consolation prize is a piece of paper that says he has to stay one five hundred feet away from me? The fact that I am supposed to be OK with this is mind-blowing! This is why those caught in domestic violence don't come forward. What's the point?"

At the conclusion of her monologue, Ann stood up and stormed out. Brooke had never wanted to high-five another person more than she did Ann Reese in that moment. Ann's parents quickly rose from the table, glared at Brian, then followed their daughter through the large door.

"I did not see that coming," Beal said under his breath.

"She's not wrong," Brooke responded so everyone could hear.

Brian seemed annoyed. "She might not be wrong, but that is the law. I'll see you all in twenty minutes when they call us in. I am going to go brief the defendant and his attorney."

Brooke hoped the bravery Ann had shown would stick with her, as the worst was still to come: now she had to face her husband in court.

CHAPTER 17

Brooke found Ann in the tiled hallway by the courtroom, tucked into a corner with her family, crying quietly. She stood in front of her and kneeled down to her level. "You aren't wrong," she said. "You and I both know that. So does everyone here. I am so sorry there isn't more that can be done right now."

"Maybe when I am in a body bag, someone will finally do something." Ann got up and walked toward the ladies' restrooms.

Brooke felt awful—this whole thing was awful. She did not blame Ann for being mad at every person in there, especially those who had told her they'd help her. Brooke felt as if she had let Ann down, and on top of that, she was worried for the woman's safety.

Twenty minutes later, everyone filed into the courtroom. Ann was led in first, then Brooke, who sat in the back. Don Reese and his attorney, Greg Levine, came next. Don gave off an air of arrogance—he looked like the cat who ate the bird but didn't want to swallow it. His eyes darted from Ann to Greg and then back again as Greg whispered in his ear.

Brian, seated at the table on the right, stood and addressed the judge when it was time. He recounted the events of the night when Ann and the kids fled to safety.

Brooke looked at Ann. She had her head down, staring toward her lap, and her shoulders shook with emotion. She couldn't imagine how hard this was for her, to hear the events of that evening shared in court and still know nothing was going to happen to her estranged and violent husband. When Brooke looked at Don, he was clutching his chest and his face had turned red. *Is he sobbing?*

Brian finished, and the judge addressed Greg Levine: "Counselor, how does your client plead?"

Greg stood and buttoned his jacket. "Thank you, Your Honor." He motioned for his client to stand up.

Don obliged. "I plead no contest," Don said quietly. *No contest? He even gets away with not pleading guilty!*

"What does the Commonwealth suggest?" the judge asked Brian.

"The Commonwealth is seeking the first offender disposition for the defendant, Mr. Reese, and is granting Mrs. Reese a permanent protective order."

The judge addressed Greg Levine again. "Counselor?"

"No objections, Your Honor."

It took another couple of minutes for the judge to process the protective order and divvy up the rest of the paperwork. Then that was it. Ann and her parents walked out first, followed by Officer Palasco. Don Reese left shortly thereafter, along with Greg Levine, who stopped next to Brooke on his way out. "I hope we can have a little more professional courtesy on our next case, Detective Hill," he said. Before waiting for a reply, he marched out with this bag over his shoulder.

Jerk, Brooke thought as she stood up.

Standing with Beal just outside the courtroom moments later, Brooke couldn't unclench her fists. Beal wore a grimace.

"That was frustrating," he said.

"You're telling me."

"Do you want me to call off the patrols?"

"No—keep them up for now. I know it sounds crazy, but I want to keep this going. I need to make sure Ann is safe."

"Honestly, I agree with you." He turned to face Brooke. He gave a half-smile meant to encourage her.

"Thanks, Dan. I'll see you later. Give Kat a hug for me." Brooke dismissed him with a nod.

As she walked away, she looked down at her phone and saw a text from Brian: *Can you wait five minutes before leaving? I'm just wrapping up in here with the judge.*

I guess being a Commonwealth attorney allows you to have the privilege of having your cell phone on, Brooke thought. She sat down on one of the empty benches outside the courtroom. As she rested her back against the wall with her eyes closed, Don Reese approached her. "Detective Hill?"

Brooke stood up. There was no way she was going to let this man tower over her. "Mr. Reese. What can I do for you?" she asked as she stood up.

"I wanted to thank you."

Brooke felt confused. "Thank me? May I ask what for?" Adrenaline pumped through her heart, setting off warning bells in her gut.

"I understand you've gone out of your way to help my wife. This has been difficult for the entire family, and I really appreciate you doing that." He frowned and looked at the floor.

Brooke wasn't sure how to react, but she assumed this must be part of his act. She'd seen it before—the manipulation, the feigned humility. This guy didn't have a genuine bone in his body, and she was going to prove it. She just wished she could figure out his angle quickly—before it was too late.

"You're right; domestic violence affects the entire family. My job is to protect and help the abused, even beyond the court hearings." It was a not-so-veiled warning—*I'm watching you,* is what Brooke wanted to say. *Just like you're watching Ann.*

"I understand you have personal experience with that, Detective." A slight grin escaped Don's mouth before it vanished as quickly as it had come.

How in the world does he know that? She was about to respond— perhaps with a punch to his jaw—when she heard her name.

"Detective, you ready to go?" Brian appeared behind Don. *He is a superhero!*

"Yes." She turned back to look Don Reese in the eyes. "Goodbye, Mr. Reese." She moved past him and didn't look back.

"What was that about?" Brian turned to watch Don Reese walk the other direction, then focused back on Brooke.

"I don't know, but I do not trust that man. I have to be honest with you, Brian; I'm frustrated that he got off. He's going to hurt that woman—I know it. I can feel it in my bones." She tried to breathe normally as they walked, but her anger was surging.

"I get what you are saying, I do. If I could have gone after him for more, I would have—you have to know that. Our laws are built to give some grace to first-time offenders in this area, with the hope they make better decisions next time."

"I know. I'm not upset with you. I'm just upset with the system… more than upset."

"How about I buy you dinner tonight, and we can commiserate?" Brian asked, touching Brooke's arm and stopping to face her. His freshly shaved face looked so soft that she could've reached up and stroked it.

"I would love to, but my little sister is in town. Raincheck?" Brooke felt torn between her feelings and attraction to two men. On one hand, she had Nick, the guy whom she'd always thought of as her ruggedly hot friend with the surfer vibe, relaxed attitude, and rotating girlfriends. On the other, she had Superman, the trustworthy attorney, the poster child for "tall, dark, and handsome." Part of her regretted chasing Brian down last night, but another part of her agreed with Jacs: what did she have to lose?

"Absolutely," he said, kissing her cheek. "Until next time. And by the way, you should wear dresses and heels like that more often. You look gorgeous." He winked before rounding the corner and disappearing.

Brooke smiled at the compliment and pulled out her phone. There was a text from Cassie: *On my way! Can you get off early?*

Brooke could not think of a better way to end this awful day than with time alongside her bubbly younger sister. She just hoped she had the energy to keep up with her.

CHAPTER 18

When Brooke opened the door to her home, she saw Cassie opening a bottle of wine with Jacs in the kitchen.

"We are so fighting!" Cassie yelled as she tackled Brooke in the mudroom with a fierce hug that swallowed Brooke whole.

"Seems like it!" Brooke laughed and wrapped her arms around Cassie.

"First, I was annoyed that you didn't call me last night after your big talk with Nick. Then—" Cassie said, taking a big dramatic breath, "Jacs told me you had sex with him! I am so proud of you!" Cassie held out her hand for a high-five, which Brooke nonchalantly accepted.

"Thanks, I guess. It just sort of happened."

Cassie looked at her eagerly. Brooke, knowing that look, sighed. "I will be happy to share all the juicy details, but I need time to decompress after court today."

"Fair enough. What happened today? He got off, didn't he? I can see it all over your face." Cassie moved to sit next to Jacs on the couch in the family room. The mid-afternoon sunlight was streaming in on the two of them as they waited for Brooke to continue.

"He did, which honestly makes sense since it is his first offense. It's just... there is something about him. I don't think he's done messing with that poor woman. I really hope my gut is wrong." Brooke sat down on the leather chair opposite Cassie and Jacs.

Jacs bounced up, ran to the kitchen, and when she came back, she handed Brooke a glass of the red blend the two had opened. "When has your gut ever been wrong?"

Cassie raised her glass. "Right, well I am very proud of my big sister for going balls to the wall on her first big case as a hot-shot detective… as well as *finally* sleeping with Officer Hottie. This calls for a toast!"

There's that energy I knew I need.

"Cheers to our fierce Detective Hill!" Jacs yelled. The three of them leaned forward and clinked glasses.

———

Before Brooke realized it, they were three bottles down, and it was only 6:00 p.m. Cassie decided she needed to take a "*siesta*"—her word—on the couch, and Jacs disappeared to the balcony to talk on the phone with some guy she was seeing. Brooke pulled out her phone. There was a text from Nick: *You forget about me?*

Brooke immediately called him, and he picked up on the first ring. "How could I ever forget about you?" Brooke said before he had a chance to say hello.

"I am pretty unforgettable." He chuckled on the other end.

She smiled. "What are you doing?"

"Just got home. You?"

"Jacs and Cassie are here." Brooke was doing her best to sound as sober as possible, but she knew by her slurred speech that she was failing.

"Ah, that explains your wine voice."

"I… just come over." The words tumbled out of her mouth before she had the chance to weigh them.

"And interrupt girls' night?"

"It's not really—at least not anymore. Jacs is talking to some guy on the phone, which means she is about to leave. And Cassie is already passed out on the couch, which means in about two hours, she will head back to Aunt T's and crawl into bed. Just come over."

"We do need to talk," Nick reminded her.

"I believe you were the one who said talking was overrated." Brooke couldn't help the flirtatious response. But then she bit her lip—*too far?* Brian's face popped into her head.

But it was too late. The flirty ask won over Nick, and twenty minutes later, he was knocking on her door. In another ten, he was in Brooke's bed with her. As predicted, Jacs had left right before Nick showed up, and at some point, Cassie left too. Brooke was hoping before heading to Aunt T's, Cassie hadn't heard too much—the walls were not that thick.

"I take it you forgive me now?" Nick asked as he rolled over onto his side to look at Brooke.

Crap, Brooke thought. *So much for being strong.* "I don't know that *forgive* is the right word, but I am choosing to believe you."

"I'll take that."

"It's over with her?" Brooke couldn't bring herself to say Liv's name.

"Yes. Promise."

As Brooke kissed him again, her phone buzzed. "Hang on—sorry. I have to take this."

The name on her screen was Ann Reese. Brooke punched the green phone icon. "Ann? Are you OK?" Brooke sat up, wrapping her sheet around her, feeling a sense of déjà vu. Hearing Ann's name put Nick on alert, too, and he sat up next to her. For reasons unknown to her, Brooke put the phone on speaker.

"Um, I'm not sure," Ann answered. "I'm getting weird messages." Her voice was still strong, and Brooke felt some measure of relief for that.

"Weird, like how?" Brooke asked. She looked at Nick, whose head was now on her shoulder.

"Pat is here. I'm going to put him on the phone. I think he can explain everything better."

"Detective Hill?" Officer Palasco said into the phone. Brooke could hear the concern in his voice.

"Yes. What's going on?"

"We were sitting here at Ann's house, and she started getting alerts on her phone. Someone named Tyler Moore is messaging her on Facebook. She doesn't know him, and when we looked him up, his profile appears to be brand new. I'm thinking a fake."

"OK…"

"He messaged Ann that she better check into her new man—this guy's words—because he has had a different girl at his place every night. And then this person went on to ask if we really thought Don would want someone like me around his kids."

"Is there any way you can send me a screenshot of those messages?" Brooke was wracking her brain, trying to figure out how to get to the bottom of this. She was sure Don was behind this—or at least, had someone doing this on his behalf.

"Yeah, not a problem; Ann took screenshots of everything. She also blocked this Tyler Moore person and reported the account as a fake account. I was going to call my station's IT person to see if they can start looking into this, but thought we'd better call you to see how to proceed."

"Let's keep it all at my station, if you don't mind. Can you put Ann back on the phone?"

"Brooke?" Ann said between tears.

"Ann, when we get off the phone, send me the screenshots. Follow Officer Palasco's instructions for blocking this person. On Monday morning, I am going to turn this over to our IT person and see what we can find out. Maybe disable your account for the weekend? For sure the notifications. Just to give you some peace of mind?" Brooke looked over at Nick, who was still listening intently next to her. He raised an eyebrow.

"Yes, I think I'll do that," Ann said. "Thank you, Brooke. I'll speak to you on Monday."

Brooke threw her phone down and growled. "That man!"

"Easy, Hill, it will be OK." Nick slid an arm around her waist.

"I know that monster Don Reese is stalking his wife, and now it's through Facebook. I'm so frustrated with Brian for not giving him more than a slap on the wrist!"

"Who's Brian?" Nick sat up straighter, looking at Brooke.

As soon as he asked, she knew she had said too much by using his first name. She turned and looked at Nick. "The lawyer."

"Brooke. Brian who?" His tone was more serious this time. It seemed Nick could sense there was more to the story than just being on a first-name basis with one of the Commonwealth attorneys.

"He's the Commonwealth attorney who prosecuted Don Reese today. I went to college with him and," Brooke paused before continuing, "funnily enough, he asked me out."

"He asked you out? In college? Or recently?" Nick asked. He moved toward the edge of the bed while still staring at her.

"Um, yeah, recently." Brooke felt nervous. "Two nights ago." *Why did I have to say that?* she thought. *Too late to back out now.*

"Two nights ago? Really? Interesting...what did you say?" Nick started to get up and put on his clothes. Brooke debated how to answer, but she knew she wasn't going to lie. After all, Nick was the one whose former flame answered his phone.

"Brooke, what did you say?" Nick said, pressing her. His face showed a mixture of hurt and anger.

"I said no… at first. Then I called you, and Liv picked up. So then I said yes." Brooke looked at him, but now could not read his expression.

"Interesting."

"What do you mean by that? You keep saying *interesting*."

Nick put his shoes on. "I think I should probably go."

"Wait, Nick. Please don't go." Brooke reached out to grab his arm, but he pulled it away from her.

"Look, like you said, this is fun, but I am under no impression that I'm your boyfriend." The words stung, and she knew she had hurt him. Brooke had to look away to keep the tears welling up in her eyes at bay.

"I thought you weren't taking what happened seriously, or that what had happened was a one-time deal for you… I don't know what I thought at that moment," she whispered.

"Do you honestly think that little of me that I would sleep with you and think it was nothing? Jeez, Brooke, it's like you are completely ignoring the fact I have been in love with you for the past five years!" He was shouting now, but then he suddenly stopped himself. "I need to go."

Brooke couldn't hold the tears back any longer. "Nick, wait! Come on! I did not go on a date with him. I didn't kiss him, and we—you and I—are not official. We haven't even discussed, well, whatever this is! We still haven't had that talk!" Brooke was yelling now, too, as she followed him to the front door.

"I know that." He opened the door and turned to face her. "I know that I have no right to be as angry as I am. But I am, and I… I just can't believe you could think I would, for even one minute, think this—" He pointed back and forth between the two of them. "You and me, was nothing."

Then he strode out the door and didn't look back.

CHAPTER 19

Once more, Brooke was destined for a restless night's sleep. She kept replaying her conversation with Nick, and when her mind was not on that, it was on Don Reese. Brooke's gut was rarely wrong, and it was telling her this guy was up to something. The Facebook messages were an escalation in her mind. But he was smart; Brooke gave him that. Don was doing just enough to scare his wife but not enough to pin anything on him. When Brooke's eyes finally slid closed, she wished they hadn't…

———

It's so hot! She can't breathe!

"Cass, we gotta back up."

The sound of sirens fills the inky black air.

Suddenly, a gloved hand grabs her shoulder… she turns and see a giant. He's dressed in dark plastic, with hoses snaking away from him.

Cassie screams.

But his face is kind. "Come on, girls. This way." The hand directs them toward another siren, blaring from a white box-shaped truck—it's an ambulance.

Before we reach it, she turns and looks at their house. All she sees is orange. All she hears is the popping of the flames. All she wants is Mommy! She should have...

Brooke bolted upright in bed, her heart racing inside her chest and her left leg feeling numb. Much like the other times Brooke felt stress, the nightmares from her childhood had enveloped her. She glanced at the clock: 7:04. *Saturday morning.* She was shaking, but all she could remember from this latest dream was the feeling of the fire, the *sound* of the fire, and the longing to do something. *But what?*

With no more details coming, she waved the proverbial white flag and got out of bed. Her leg still felt the pins and needles of being tucked underneath her at an awkward angle during the dream, so she limped into the bathroom, her phone in hand.

She texted Aunt T to see if she wanted to go for a run. Two minutes later, Aunt T texted back: *Love to! 9:00? Our usual spot? I'll leave Cassie a note.*

A decompressing run and coffee with Aunt T were just what Brooke needed to help clear her mind of Nick and the dream, and maybe gain some clarity on how to proceed with the Reese case. And Brian.

Two hours later, Brooke was hugging Aunt T at their habitual running location, Gravelly Point Park. Because it was located next to National Airport, it was often crowded with airplane enthusiasts—Aunt T loved to run at the park, and found watching the planes a serene bonus to the grueling exercise.

Brooke noticed her aunt's lean body underneath her running attire. *Hope I look that fit at her age!*

As they started jogging, it didn't take long for Aunt T to probe Brooke about what was going on. "We can keep talking about the weather; I can keep asking questions, or you can go ahead and just spit whatever it is out and save us both some time."

As usual, with the not-so-gentle prodding from her mother's sister, everything came out. Brooke mentioned Nick's name briefly, but she spilled everything about Brian's date proposal, Ann's stalker, the court's decision, and her nightmares. She held nothing back. Aunt T had to direct Brooke to a nearby bench so Brooke could catch her breath and dry her eyes.

"This case… it has so many similarities to what happened to us, Aunt T." Brooke blew her nose as her aunt sat down next to her. "I just feel like I have really let this woman down. You should have seen the way she looked at me yesterday in court. I swore I would do everything in my power to help people—people like her, especially—so they didn't suffer the same fate my mother did." She couldn't help it; the tears were freely flowing now.

"'People like her.' You mean, people like you?" Aunt T said as put her hand on Brooke's arm and scooted closer on the bench. "Sweetheart, you *have* helped—and you can't change the system all in one day and with one case." Aunt T looked for another tissue in her shorts pocket. After finding one, she handed it to Brooke.

Brooke blew her nose. "I know that; I do. I just worry that because I couldn't do more, something will happen to her or to her children." She sighed and looked far off into the distance.

"Brooke, she's not your mom."

"I know. It's just—"

Aunt T put her hand up in protest and cut her off. "No, sweetheart, listen to me: this woman is not your mother. You can't act out this fantasy anymore."

"What do you mean?" Brooke blew her nose again.

"When you were little, after everything that happened, I took you and Cass to therapy. You know what the therapist used to say to me? She told me Cassie would seek solace in her creativity, which I think we can agree is true, but she said you... you would always fantasize about how, even at five years old, you could have saved your mother." Aunt T tucked one of Brooke's loose hairs behind her ear, just as she always had, ever since Brooke was a child.

"Do you think that's what I'm doing?" Brooke looked wide-eyed at her aunt, preparing herself for the answer.

"I think you are in danger of doing that, yes. I worry with this case that you are being too hard on yourself. Brooke, you could not have saved your mother, and you have done everything you can for this woman. You need to realize that or you're not going to make it in this role... this career." Aunt T put her arm around Brooke and hugged her to her side.

Brooke looked down at the ground. "Maybe you're right."

"Oh, I'm definitely right. You just have to choose to believe it." Aunt T flipped her hair, trying to bring levity to the conversation.

"Choose to believe it," Brooke repeated, thinking back to Nick and how she had chosen to believe him about Liv.

"Penny for your thoughts?"

"I'm just processing what you said." Brooke watched the distant planes taking off, part of her wishing she could fly somewhere far, far away. *But who would I want to run away with?*

"OK. Well, while you process, let's head down to the corner coffee shop. I'm dying for some caffeine." Aunt T stood up, holding out her hand for Brooke to join her.

They stood up and started to jog together again. Both were silent. Brooke's mind was racing, and she suspected Aunt T was only quiet because she was allowing Brooke to think about what she had just said.

As they headed into the coffee shop, Brooke glanced at her phone. Nothing. She expected to have a text from Nick, and when one wasn't there, she felt a pull on her heartstrings. Her biggest fear was losing him, both as a boyfriend *and* as a friend, but she was wrestling inside her head with which one was more important to her.

"Would you like to talk about Nick now or leave that alone?" Aunt T nodded toward Brooke's phone screen, and Brooke looked at her with surprise. *Can she read my mind?*

"Don't look so shocked—you mentioned him on the run, but Cassie came home last night and told me everything."

"I should have known. She doesn't know everything, though. Nick didn't leave on the best terms last night. I'm just wondering where things stand." Liquid emotion rimmed her eyes again.

"Maybe you both need a bit of space to gain some clarity. Remember, space and time are not always your enemies." Aunt T handed Brooke her coffee as she sipped hers.

Brooke nudged her with her arm. "Yes, I know. You have told me that many times."

After their coffees, they said farewell, and Aunt T hugged her. "I'll see you tomorrow at Carol and Ben's. Go easy on yourself, Brooke. In both your professional and personal lives."

"Thanks, Aunt T, I appreciate it. I'm fine." Brooke gave her a return hug.

When she got back into her car, she checked her phone. Still nothing from Nick. She wasn't sure if she should reach out to him or wait for him to reach out to her, but halfway through her short drive home, she decided to text him. She activated her Bluetooth and spoke into the air: *I don't know how to navigate this. I want to talk when you are ready.*

Then she said a prayer and tapped the send icon.

CHAPTER 20

When Brooke arrived home, Cassie was already there, standing in her foyer with her hands on her hips and a determined look on her face. "We are going out," she proclaimed.

"No. I just got back from a run with Aunt T, and after the week I've had, the last thing I feel like doing is going out. That is a firm no." Brooke shook her head and walked toward the shower.

Cassie smiled before she replied. "I figured it was a no; I was just testing you. I'm guessing work is hitting you hard and things did not go as well as you wanted with Nick last night?"

Brooke turned and nodded begrudgingly. Cassie continued: "I brought some champagne over. We are going to sit on your couch, drink, watch Netflix, and order takeout. You can talk or be quiet, whatever you want. Just know I am here, and I am not leaving."

"Cassie. It's not even lunchtime?"

"Who cares? You gotta relax. And we don't have to start with the champagne until five o'clock if you really care that much."

Brooke teared up and walked toward her sister to give her a tight hug. "I love you, Cass. Thank you for being you."

"You would do the same for me. Now go take a shower—you stink." Cassie's nose scrunched up as she shooed Brooke away.

———

As nighttime rolled around, and Cassie, sound asleep next to her on the couch, breathed deeply, Brooke finally felt herself relax. She had checked her phone obsessively all day, but there was nothing from Nick. At ten, she tucked Cassie under some blankets on the couch and headed for bed.

As she was drifting off to sleep, her phone buzzed. She rolled toward the bedside table and picked it up. It was Nick: *I'm such an idiot. I have no right to be mad at you, and I had no right to storm off like that.*

Brooke sat up and typed a return message. *I should not have said anything. I feel like it became something when it's really nothing.*

It felt like an eternity before Nick responded: *I don't think we can put this off much longer; we need to talk soon. Let's get some breathing room and meet in a few days. Does that work?*

Remembering Aunt T's words, Brooke agreed, then rolled over, pulled her duvet above her head, and closed her eyes.

———

At two o'clock in the morning, Brooke's phone buzzed again with a phone call, waking her up from a deep sleep. She answered without looking at the caller ID, assuming it was Nick again.

"Hello?" Her voice sounded groggy, and she cleared her throat before saying hello again.

A whispered voice snapped her to alert. "Brooke," Ann said. "Don's here! He's trying to break in the back door!"

"I'm on my way. Hang up and dial 911! And hide! I'll be there soon." Brooke jumped out of bed, ran to her bedroom door, and flicked the switch. Her room was bathed in the bright white light of her mini chandelier. She grabbed a pair of blue jeans and a black T-shirt and threw the T-shirt over her head. Then she wrestled with her jeans. Her toe caught in the rip in the knee as she pushed her second leg through, and she cursed. Finally, Brooke picked up her gun and phone from her bedside table and ran into the kitchen to find her shoes. There wasn't time to leave a note for Cass, who was still snoring on the couch. *I'll text her later.*

After sprinting to her car and pressing the ignition button, the tires on her Camry squealed as she tore out of her driveway. Brooke didn't even bother with her seat belt.

Hang on, Ann!

CHAPTER 21

"911, what's your emergency?"

"He's here! He's trying to get into the house! Oh, my gosh… please, help me!"

"Ma'am, calm down. What is your name?

"Ann Reese. My kids are here with me."

"Can you give me your location, Ann?"

"My house! He's messing with me! He kept appearing and reappearing at windows. Now he's banging on the back door! I can't do this! Please, send someone!"

"Who is at the windows, ma'am?"

"My husband. I have a protective order against him. Please… the alarm keeps going off, and my kids are screaming. Please, please send someone quickly!"

"Ma'am, I am dispatching the police right now. Just stay on the phone with me. Where do you see him?"

"I looked out the front door earlier, and he was standing in the driveway, so I ran and turned the alarm on. Then I ran to the back door, and he was standing there, right at the door. I screamed; the kids screamed, and we all ran upstairs and locked ourselves in my bathroom. Now the alarm is going off. We hear banging on the door, like he's using an ax or crowbar or something!"

"You said your alarm is going off?"

"Yes, can't you hear it?"

"Yes, but I do not have it registered in our system. Do you know if it is wired to alert the police and fire department?"

"What? How is that possible? It's supposed to notify you!"

"Ma'am, have you had anyone come out to service the system recently?"

"Oh my—"

"Ma'am, what happened? Did something happen?"

"He must've broken into the alarm system!"

"It's OK. I'm right here, ma'am. Help is on the way. Where is he now?"

"I know he planned this! He is going to break down our door! He's going to kill me! Where are the police? They should be here!"

"Ma'am, they're on their way. A few minutes out."

Silence.

"Ma'am?"

Dial tone.

———

Brooke spied Ann's house through her windshield. The lights were off in the home, and she couldn't see anything out of the ordinary from the street—the place looked secure. She pulled into the driveway and slammed on the brakes. After jumping out of her car, she ran toward the front door. Grasping the door handle, she gave it a good push. It didn't budge.

Locked! Shoot!

Brooke looked around for any sign of people or a forced entry. *Nothing.* She didn't ring the doorbell because she heard the alarm blaring inside, and she didn't think anyone would hear the doorbell over the ruckus—and she didn't want to alert Don to her presence. She grabbed her gun from the back waistband of her jeans and rounded the corner of the house, heading for the back door. Her weapon was raised, and she propped a flashlight on the top of it with her other hand to light the path through the dark.

As she entered the backyard, she heard banging and grunting. In the glow of the spotlight, she spied Don, dressed in all black, pounding on the back door handle and frame with a hammer. The wood was splintering, the door nearly ready to give way.

"Police! Stop right there, Don Reese! You're under arrest!" Brooke screamed, aiming the gun at his back.

Don turned to glare at her, the hammer still gripped in his fist, hanging at his side. Sweat beaded on his brow and the front of his shirt and under his armpits looked wet. His eyes were wild.

"Drop the hammer! Then turn and put your hands on the back of your head!" Brooke yelled.

Don laughed and bent down, dropping the hammer onto the ground. But as the tool hit the cement pavers below his feet, he reached behind his back with his other hand and pulled a gun, turning it on Brooke.

In an instant, Brooke heard the telltale *bang!* just milliseconds before she felt a burning pain sear through her left shoulder. At the same time that her body jerked backward, her academy training and reflexes kicked in, and she aimed her weapon toward Don, firing as she fell to the ground.

———

Upstairs in the bathroom, huddled behind a locked door, Ann hugged her kids as she spoke to the 911 operator. Suddenly, Ann realized the banging had stopped. Ann took the phone away from her ear to better hear what Don was up to now.

In the next instant, a gunshot rang out in the backyard. It was quickly followed by another. Ann gripped the phone, accidentally hanging up on the operator. She threw it on the ground and screamed for her children to get into the bathtub and lay down. She threw some towels over them, hiding them from view.

"Don't move until I come get you!" Ann directed her trembling children.

"Mommy! Don't go!" Connor whimpered.

"It'll be OK, honey. Emma, stay with Connor." The kids held hands, and Ann felt her heart shatter.

Turning from her precious children, Ann pulled a pair of grooming scissors from her vanity drawer. Gripping them tightly, she slowly opened the bathroom door. Everything was quiet—even the alarm had stopped sounding.

Ann moved toward her bed and bent down. She retrieved her old field hockey stick from her high school days, which she had stashed under her bed days before for protection. Now she had two weapons.

As she tiptoed down the stairs in her bare feet, she heard police sirens approaching her house. But she couldn't breathe a sigh of relief yet: *Was someone hurt? What were the gunshots for?*

When Ann reached the back door, she spied Brooke, sitting in the light cast by the backyard spotlight, another officer running toward her. Brooke was holding her hand to her shoulder, and Ann saw the blood seeping across Brooke's fingers.

A whimper escaped Ann's throat. As she continued to assess the situation, she realized that other than the shoulder wound, Brooke appeared to be OK; she was awake and talking to the other officer.

But Don was nowhere to be seen.

CHAPTER 22

Benji and Carol Noble's house was straight out of Old Town New England. There was a fireplace in every room, and everything was decorated with a nod to the Colonial American era. It was the coziest house Brooke had ever been in, and she loved coming here.

Carol greeted Brooke and Cassie at the door and ushered them inside. Carol was the epitome of the Southern belle—she had followed Benji from Georgia to Virginia after they were married, and her "Deep Peach" accent had never wavered. She liked to remind people that Virginia, even Northern Virginia, was still very much part of the South. "Come on in! Brooke, how are you doing?" Carol's eyes showed genuine concern, her mouth a twisted line across her lower face.

Brooke had called Benji from Inova Alexandria Hospital around 4:00 A.M., just before she was discharged. He had raced there and then drove her home afterward, since Brooke hadn't notified Cassie of her injury yet. Brooke had wanted to see her in person when she heard the news so that she would know Brooke was OK. *No use in worrying her*, Brooke had reasoned.

The bullet had just nicked her left shoulder and required only a few stitches. Humiliation was the bigger hurt: Don had gotten away. She said as much to Lieutenant Adams when she'd arrived by her bedside in the Emergency Room to check on her. The Lieutenant had waved her off, saying they'd find Don soon.

"I'm doing perfectly fine," Brooke confirmed to Carol. "A flesh wound, as we like to say." She smiled to prove she was not dying. Cassie glared at her, still feeling the betrayal of Brooke not calling her first.

"Talia and I are just opening our second bottle of wine." Carol waved for them to follow her.

"Did she just say *second* bottle of wine?" Brooke whispered to Cassie as she grabbed her sister's arm in another show of apology. Cassie relented, and the two walked arm in arm toward the kitchen, allowing Carol to lead them to the other voices wafting through the house.

"Yup. I guess we know what kind of Sunday night I am going to have. Not you, though; you're on those hefty pain meds." They giggled like middle school girls, the tension broken by the feelings of gratitude and the cozy home in which they found themselves.

Inside the massive kitchen, they found Aunt T and Benji seated at the long wooden farm-style table. Aunt T stood immediately.

"Brooke!" Aunt T hugged her carefully. "I'm so glad you're all right. We were all so worried!"

"Yup, I'm fine—I just wish Don Reese didn't get away."

Everyone nodded, knowing the situation was far from over. Benji motioned to Brooke. "This one deserves a big glass of wine after the night she's had."

"Thanks. My first case has certainly been rough, but I was expecting the job to be like this. I'm really fine." She gave a knowing look to Benji. "And I can't have the wine, thank you… pain medication and all." She smirked and raised her arm, wincing as it got above ninety degrees. "At least I don't need a sling."

Carol looked at her, sympathy draping her face. "Oh, I remember some of the cases Benji worked over the years. I remember some so vividly, even though I wasn't even the one working them—I can't believe what ya'll go through with these DV calls—but Brooke, Benji was never shot!"

Brooke nodded and chuckled. "I'm always aiming to one-up him." She bit her lip, realizing she now wanted to change the topic—she'd had enough of her job and this case for one weekend. "The house smells amazing, Carol! I thought you were making meatloaf?" Brooke asked.

Benji nodded from the stool he was perched on, keeping quiet.

Carol answered Brooke. "I did. I made meatloaf with some sides and baked a pecan pie for y'all." She moved around the massive kitchen in her red and white checkered apron as if a meal like this was no trouble at all.

Aunt T raised her glass. "She's making it sound easy. She made everything from scratch, including the rolls. I know because I have been providing moral support all day."

"Cassie, how are the auditions going? Talia was starting to tell me, but I want to hear from you," Carol asked, still mixing various foods inside the pans on the stove.

Before Cassie could answer, Brooke's phone rang Aunt T raised her glass, it was Nick. She silenced it. She had texted him once she had arrived at the hospital, letting him know she was fine after the "officer-involved shooting" he likely heard broadcast over the communications channels. She assumed the fact it was her who'd been shot would spread faster than ice melting at the equator. She had asked Nick to wait before contacting her so she could get treated and get some sleep, and had even sent him a picture of the six stitches before the physician's assistant had bandaged her up, but now was not a good time for conversation with Nick either.

"Auditions are going OK," Cassie answered Carol. "Some are better than others. The problem is the director or playwright always has this vision of what they want, so even when I think I'm perfect for the part, I might not have the right look. It's just so—oh my gosh! Can you both please just pick up your phones!"

Both Brooke and Benji's phones were ringing now. "It's Simons." Benji said, as he picked up.

Brooke looked at hers. It was Beal. "Dan, what's up?"

"Brooke, we just got an all-units call to another domestic disturbance at the Reese residence. I'm about a minute away. No details other than we're assuming Don is back. Not sure how he got past the surveillance we put in place since last night."

"I'm leaving now." Brooke hung up as Benji disconnected with Nick.

"That was Simons looking for you about the Reese case."

"I know. There is something going on at the Reese residence again! Carol, Cassie, Aunt T, I am so sorry, but I have to go." Brooke ran toward the front door, not bothering to look back.

Benji grabbed his keys and followed Brooke. "I'll drive."

There was no time to argue with him. Cassie had driven her to the Nobles' home, and she needed to get to Ann quickly.

As Benji sped across town, Brooke couldn't help but wonder why Don would try to go back—he was a wanted man, after all *Why risk it? Especially after he'd shot an officer—me!*

But she wasn't worried about herself, though — she worried about what they might find when they arrived at the Reeses' home.

CHAPTER 23

The sun was making its nightly descent, its bottom tip now hiding below the horizon, creating an orange glow. Benji and Brooke arrived at the Reese residence in record time. What they found was a different scene from the previous night, when Brooke had arrived by herself in the inky blackness of the early morning hours. Now there was a sea of police cars, a fire truck, and an ambulance blocking the cul-de-sac, their lights adding to nature's colorful display.

Benji was forced to park at the top of the street. Brooke jumped out of the car and ran toward the Reese residence, holding her injured arm against her body to help prevent the flashes of pain the jostling created.

"Brooke!"

She stopped at the sound of Nick's voice. He was standing in the Reeses' driveway, dressed in his uniform. She made a beeline toward him.

"What's going on? Are they OK?" Brooke realized she was frantic and tried to calm her nerves.

She was grateful Nick got right to the point. "Ann and the kids are safe. Shaken up, but safe." He motioned to one of the police cars. "Don is in the back of that cruiser over there. Beal just read him his rights." Nick eyed her shoulder, then looked into her eyes. She assumed he wanted to ask about her and her injury.

Brooke nodded to him as she found the police car. She noticed the top of Don's head leaning against the back window. His bravado was gone, and he looked shaken up. She turned back to Nick and reached for his elbow. A peace offering, she hoped.

"I'm OK, Nick. Promise. The bullet just grazed my shoulder. You saw the picture—I'm embarrassed to have needed a visit to the hospital. We'll talk soon. Now, where are Ann and the kids? I need to make sure they're OK."

"Over there." Nick pointed toward the neighbor's house. She turned her head and saw Ann talking to Beal in the next-door neighbor's front yard. She thanked Nick and took the first few steps toward them—and that's when she saw Mr. Murray standing in the street, talking to two other officers, presumably the ones who'd been on surveillance. Mr. Murray wore camo pants and a gray T-shirt. His beard was no less scraggly than the first time Brooke saw him.

What's he doing? Brooke wondered.

Before Brooke could decide who to approach first, Ann saw her and rushed over. "Oh, Brooke!" The two women hugged, and Ann began to sob.

"Ann, I am so sorry—this has been such a nightmare. Are you OK?" Brooke glanced around. "Where are the kids?"

"The kids are inside with Pat. He's setting them up in the spare room with a movie and snacks so they don't have to be a part of all of this any more than they already have been." Ann tried to dry her eyes with her sleeve. "I'm scheduling counseling for them ASAP… and for me."

"That's a good idea, Ann. You'll all be OK." Brooke's heart was exploding in her chest, knowing first-hand what the kids were going through, but the thought of Don behind bars eased much of her anxiety.

Beal approached and leaned in toward the two women. He whispered, "Let's move into the house to talk, where prying eyes are fewer. I've called Brandon Evans in for the IT stuff."

Evans? IT stuff? Brandon Evans was their lead forensic technology specialist. Brooke wondered looked around at all the neighbors congregating on their front porches, trying to gather more information about what had disrupted their quiet evening.

When Ann, Brooke, and Beal entered the house, she found Officer Patrick Palasco holding a bowl of popcorn and standing halfway up the stairs. He was dressed in jeans and a striped button-down shirt. Brooke noticed his socked feet right away. *Quite casual!* She also saw Ann mouth a thank you to him. The three of them sat down in the family room as Palasco disappeared from view.

Before anyone spoke, Mr. Murray ambled through the front door and sat across from Brooke on the leather couch, looking way too comfortable. He didn't say a word, and eyed her calmly.

"What's going on?" She looked from the intruder to Beal.

"Detective Hill, meet Chase Murray, tonight's hero. I'll let him explain."

"What?" Brooke did a double-take glance between the neighbor and Beal, noticing for the first time an expensive tactical watch on Mr. Murray's wrist and an empty gun holster at his waist. "I don't understand—"

"Detective Hill, I apologize for our last encounter." His tone was civilized, unlike the first time Brooke had spoken to him, when she'd approached him about his camera. "I work for… a government agency, in technology. Ever since you knocked on my door, I've been keeping an eye on the Reeses' home. Actually, ever since the first alternation between Don and Ann." Mr. Murray nodded at Ann, an apology for speaking about her as if she wasn't there.

Brooke felt the family room tilt slightly. *Surprised* didn't begin to define her current state; she had pegged Ann's neighbor as Don's cohort. But she wanted to take back control of the room—she was, after all, the detective in charge.

"OK, interesting. So what happened tonight?" Her voice was authoritative, and internally, she praised her effort toward professionalism.

Officer Beal jumped in. "Mrs. Reese, I know this is hard, but I need your full statement before I take your husband in, so let's start with you. Then Detective Hill and Mr. Murray can talk privately," Officer Beal added, knowing some information Mr. Murray shared would likely only be for Brooke to hear.

Ann took a deep breath. "The kids and I had just finished dinner. Pat was over—I was still shaken up from last night, and he offered to stay here to help me and the kids cope and feel safer. I was cleaning up in the kitchen when I remembered I wanted to make sure the front door was locked. Connor had come in from playing with some of his friends before dinner, and he's notorious for leaving the door unlocked..." Ann chuckled lightly, easing her own tension. "Sure enough, it was unlocked. I looked out into the cul-de-sac, and there he was: Don... he was standing in the bushes in front of the house, just staring at it."

She shivered. "I did a double-take and shook my head, hoping it was an illusion or some kind of flashback from last night, but it was real. Not a dream—" She clasped her hands into a fist on her lap. "I screamed for Pat to grab the kids, and I pulled out my phone to call 911. But the fire truck and police cars were already arriving. I didn't know how they got there so fast, and I didn't know where the officers who'd been in front of my house went....they caught Don..." Ann looked toward Mr. Murray as the realization hit her. "I guess it was you who called them?"

Mr. Murray offered a slight nod of his head but didn't speak.

As Ann took a minute to compose herself, Brooke squeezed her arm. Beal offered a sympathetic look too. Brooke realized how good Dan was with these types of cases.

"Ann, did you see your husband holding anything, or did he make any gesture toward you?" Brooke asked.

Ann shook her head no. "Not that I could see. I mean, he could have, but like I said, I yelled for Pat to grab the kids, and when we met at the stairs, I took them and ran upstairs. I barricaded the three of us in my bathroom again." Tears slid down her cheeks. "Just like last night. I didn't know where Pat went… I guess I assumed he was going to confront Don." She put her head in her hands and cried harder, as her worry for Pat finally hit her full force.

"I'm sorry, Ann," Brooke turned to Beal. "Have you discovered if Don had anything with him? A gun? Anything? And I want to know what happened to our surveillance team." Brooke's tone was furious.

Beal nodded. "There was a full can of gasoline sitting in the shadows of the bushes, and he had a gun on his person. No doubt, it will be a match for the bullet that nicked you last night. Once we had him handcuffed and in the cruiser, I called Mrs. Reese to let her know we were outside and to open the door." He paused before adding, "I'll find out about the surveillance team ASAP."

With the information about another gas can, Ann fell back into the armchair she was sitting in, convulsing with emotion.

The woman is losing it, and I don't blame her. "We'll get Officer Palasco's statement separately. We can be finished for now, Ann." Brooke nodded to Beal, whose serious expression matched her own, indicating it was time to go get answers and take Don to be booked at the station. "Officer Beal, can you send in someone to stay with Ann and the kids? And I'll speak with Officer Palasco after I talk with Mr. Murray here. So don't let him go anywhere. Thanks." She dismissed Beal.

Brooke turned to the curious neighbor-turned-government agent. "Let's go for a walk, Mr. *Chase* Murray."

CHAPTER 24

C hase Murray followed Brooke through the front door and over to the driveway. The sun had set completely, and the street-lights had popped on, illuminating the scene, which by this time was much less crowded. Only Benji's car and two other patrol cars remained—one was Beal's, with Don's profile still visible in the back seat. Brooke was glad he'd be heading to the magistrate within minutes. The other patrol car was Nick's, and he and Benji stood down the street talking. Brooke didn't want to even guess the topic of their discussion; she prayed it wasn't her.

"Let's stand over here," Brooke directed, striding closer to the mailbox and out of earshot of Nick, Benji, and anyone inside the Reeses' home. "So who are you? You certainly had me fooled, thinking you were the one helping Mr. Reese spy on his wife." This was no time for small talk.

"Detective Hill, I can't really talk about what I do, but I'm one of the good guys. When I saw Don slinking down the street, hiding in the darkness, and holding a gas can, I immediately called it in. I did not see the patrol cars that had been switching in and out all day. I stepped outside with my gun in case I needed to intervene before the police arrived. I've since put my gun away." He nodded toward his empty holster.

"How long have you lived here?"

"Six months."

"Did you know about the domestic violence?"

"Not until that first night Ann and the kids ran outside and Don fled after threatening to ignite the family home."

"Why didn't you tell me before?"

"I can't give you a detailed ans—"

"Let me guess... national security?"

"Something like that."

"You're a man of many words, Mr. Murray." Chase shrugged at her statement.

Brooke sighed. "Anything else you can tell... hold up!" She brushed past Chase and peered under the mailbox. "What in the..."

"That's a camera!" Chase offered.

"It sure is. I bet this is how Don was keeping tabs on everything happening with Ann and the kids." Brooke snapped a photo with her phone, ensuring the flash had worked by checking the image. Then she grabbed a tissue from her pocket and yelled for Nick to bring her an evidence bag from his car. She carefully used the tissue to pry the camera from the mailbox. It had been attached with two-sided Velcro. While the method of affixing the camera was rudimentary, the camera itself seemed advanced—waterproof at a minimum.

Nick ran up with an envelope and Brooke dropped the tiny camera inside. "Send it in for fingerprints, OK? I'll notify Evans to follow up with it... there he is now." They all turned to see a nondescript blue sedan inch its way down the street.

"Yes, ma'am—you bet." Nick nodded at Brooke and walked toward his cruiser. Before Nick got into his car, he turned around and said, "I'll call you later, Detective Hill. Be sure to pick up."

Brooke nodded in reply. Chase Murray raised an eyebrow and smirked. "That obvious?" she asked. The man of many words shrugged again.

After asking Officer Beal to wait on her for a couple more minutes so she could travel with them to the courthouse, Brooke walked Brandon Evans, who had just arrived, into Ann's home to chat. She found Ann standing in the kitchen with Pat, blowing her nose.

"Hi, Officer Palasco. Can we talk tomorrow first thing? Maybe you can come to the station?"

"Of course. I'll take my leave now... if you're OK, Ann?" He looked at her for confirmation.

"Yes. Thanks, Pat." Ann walked Pat to the door and returned to the kitchen. She turned on a few lights in the house to make things brighter. Brooke assumed it was an effort to help calm her nerves.

Brooke turned to the black gentleman standing with her. Brandon Evans was a two-decade-long staff member with the forensics department—a technology guru. He wore circular glasses, and tonight he was dressed in a dark blue suit with no tie. "Ann, this is Brandon Evans. He is our IT specialist," Brooke explained. "He's the one I was going to contact tomorrow about the Facebook messages you've been receiving."

Brooke turned to Brandon. "Officer Beal called you in early. Did you have a chance to get up to speed?"

"Facebook messages?" Evans asked. "Officer Beal mentioned a faulty alarm system that wasn't calling into fire or police dispatch."

"Yes, both, and we have a new development." She turned toward Ann, bracing for the woman's reaction. "I just found another camera attached to your mailbox. I've sent it off for fingerprints, and then,

Mr. Evans, can you follow up with it and learn as much as you can about it?"

"Of course." Brandon smiled warmly.

"You think Don did something to the alarm system *and* had a new camera installed to spy on me *and* sent me those Facebook messages?" Ann asked, grabbing more tissues.

"Yes. But Mr. Evans will be looking into it, and Officer Beal is going to take Mr. Reese to the magistrate now. I'm heading there, too. My guess is that he will be held without bail, given that he shot an officer and broke the restraining order parameters. I will be back in the morning, and I'll leave you with Mr. Evans now to tell him about the Facebook messages, OK?"

Brooke took a breath and left Mr. Evans with one final item: "After you've done your investigation, can you call the emergency line for Ann's security company? They will send a service person out. While it's our job to determine how and why her alarm is not hooked into the mainframe system, it's their job to fix it." She paused to let the instructions sink in.

Finally, Brooke reached out and touched Ann's arm. "Don will be behind bars, and now we know you have a neighbor watching out for your safety too. He's finished, Ann. Don is finished hurting you."

CHAPTER 25

"Wow, a two-officer escort," Don Reese said sarcastically as Brooke got into the backseat behind Officer Beal and next to the man who had shot her the night before. "Surprised you're back on the job, Detective."

Brooke ignored his comments. He smelled like sweat—a putrid mixture of ammonia and vinegar—and she held little respect for him.

Beal didn't look back but spoke up. "Mr. Reese, I would suggest not talking. Everything you say can and will be used against you in a court of law."

Don snickered, but it was a weak show of his old bravado. Brooke could tell he was dejected.

Her phone alerted her to a text. She aimed the screen toward the car window so Don couldn't read it. It was from Brian: *Hey. I just heard you were shot last night!!! You OK? Can I see you? I'm worried.*

Brian! I can't believe I forgot about Brian! It was not the time to type out a return message, but Brooke begged herself to remember to do that soon. As they rode in silence to the Fairfax County Courthouse, she thought about Brian, curious about the reason she had forgotten about him in all the melee.

Brooke was relieved that everyone was now safe and Don Reese would be officially charged and incarcerated—hopefully for a good long time. She worried about bail, though—would the magistrate hold him or grant him one last wish? She assumed he had the means to make an exorbitant bail amount since he owned an IT company. *Then we'll have to move Ann and the kids.*

As Beal parked in front of the large, brick courthouse, Don Reese said, "I want to call my attorney. I know I get one phone call."

Brooke smirked. "Yes; you are correct. But you'll be booked first—then you get your phone call. Even Greg Levine cannot change the process. As of right now, you are under arrest."

They escorted Don into the holding area, which was a small, white-painted brick room behind a set of bars. Only two blue benches took up space there. Brooke and Beal waited outside the courtroom to be seen by the magistrate. Thankfully, it was a slower Sunday night, and no one was waiting in front of them.

The judge on duty was Vivian Southers, who was the same judge presiding over the case the first time Don Reese was arrested. *A minor miracle!* Brooke respected the judge's no-nonsense approach. If there was anyone who was going to throw the book at Don Reese, it would be Judge Southers. Internally, she relaxed, and that's when she realized her shoulder was aching—she'd done too much today, her supposed "day off."

When they were called, Beal led Don out of the holding area and the three of them walked into the courtroom. After Beal summarized the events that had transpired, Judge Southers lowered her glasses. "Mr. Reese, weren't you just in my courtroom last week? Did I not make myself clear about what would happen if you returned?"

Don didn't even flinch. "I have been gone one week, and she already has another man in there! She won't let me see my children, and I am concerned about them! I got a report from one of the neighbors about her parenting, that they were about to call CPS on her. For the safety of my children, I was going to see for myself."

Brooke fumed from his lies. She anxiously awaited her turn to speak.

"Oh, I see," Judge Southers said. "So tampering with your wife's alarm system, appearing at her windows and doors at night, banging on the door with a hammer, and the multiple gas cans were all for the good of the children? Should we talk about *shooting an officer?*" The judge glanced at Brooke as Don shook his head in defeat.

"That was an accident." The judge laughed.

Guess I don't *need to speak*, Brooke thought.

Judge Southers continued: "I've heard enough. The court will hold Mr. Reese for forty-eight hours without bail. Bail is set for $250,000, with a release date of Tuesday evening if bail is posted."

Well, Brooke thought, *so much for no bail.*

With that, Don was led away, to be locked up in the county jail. As the officers escorted him out of the courtroom, Brooke could hear him asking when he could get his first phone call. "Sounds like he's anxious to call his high-powered attorney," Beal said to Brooke.

She smirked. "You just gave me a fantastic idea." She picked up her phone and tapped Greg Levine's name into her contacts.

He picked up on the first ring: "Greg Levine."

"Hi, Greg, this is Detective Brooke Hill. I am extending *professional courtesy…*" —Brooke's words held a healthy dose of sarcasm— "and letting you know your client, Don Reese, was just arrested again, this time for shooting an officer last night and breaking the protective order twice in the last twenty-four hours. He is being held for forty-eight hours and bail is set for $250,000. *Thought you'd want to know.*"

She tapped the red "disconnect" icon on her phone before Greg could utter another word.

"Satisfying?" Beal asked.

"Very."

CHAPTER 26

As she'd missed her ride with Benji, Beal dropped Brooke at home. It was nearing 11:30 P.M. Collapsing onto her living room couch, she pulled out her phone to text Brian. As she searched for his text, she realized she should probably call him instead. She'd been shot—he knew it was normal for people to feel concerned. She'd barely had time to talk to anyone. *Including Nick.*

"Drats!" she said.

"What?"

Brooke jumped at the sound of another voice. She turned and spied Cassie standing in the kitchen with a glass of water.

"Hey! You're back from the Nobles' house? Did you see Benji?"

Cassie nodded. "Yeah, we crossed paths in the driveway. I've been home about forty-five minutes. So..." She smiled at Brooke. "I hear the husband has been put away..."

"Yes. And he shouldn't be out for at least forty-eight hours, but we're going to hope for a long, long time with the growing evidence I'm collecting." The realization made Brooke tear up. She'd been stuffing everything for the past week, and the sudden awareness that her first tough case was almost closed unleashed the compartmentalized emotion.

"You did it, sis. You saved that woman and her kids."

Brooke sighed. *I did do it, didn't I?* But then she remembered the mailbox camera. "Well, there's one last thing to close. Two, actually— gotta match his gun to the bullet that grazed me. And we need to tie him to a new camera I found…but that's all I can say about that. Ongoing investigation and all." She winked at Cassie.

"I get it. But I'm so proud of you, Brooke—you did good!"

"Now I have to figure out what to do about Brian and Nick."

Cassie laughed. "Have you talked to Nick yet?"

"No. That's the problem. But I need to get back to Brian. I know he's worried. At least I saw Nick tonight. He knows I'm OK."

"I'll leave you to it, then. I'm heading to bed. I helped Aunt T and Carol finish off a third bottle of wine, and I'm beat. I'll see you in the morning. Oh, and I'll probably leave to head back to New York around nine. K?"

"OK. I have to be at work by seven. We can say goodbye in the morning… love you, Cass."

"Ditto." And with that, Cassie shuffled to the guest bedroom.

Brooke tapped her phone awake and swiped to her messages. She typed out a text to Brian: *Can I call you now?* Then she closed her eyes and waited for the reply.

Bzzzz.

Brooke looked at the screen as a message came in: *I just got to your house. Can I come in?*

———

Adrenaline had kept Brooke awake, and she spent most of the night staring at the ceiling and thinking of all the things she needed to get organized to make sure Don Reese spent a significant amount of time in jail. After a few hours, she got up, showered, and got dressed in a pair of black pants and a teal-colored silk blouse. Once her make-up was applied, she stepped out of the bathroom and saw Nick still asleep in her bed. She shook her head. *He is beautiful.*

After giving Cass a long hug, she left for work. She was just sitting down at her desk when Brian walked in. Last night, he'd texted Brooke back and made plans to meet her at her office first thing in the morning. He wanted in-person proof she was all right.

Even though she'd just spent the night with Nick and had firm plans to have their long-awaited chat that evening, Brian was still one of the most handsome men she'd ever laid eyes on. *Second only to Nick,* she thought a split-second later.

"Hey," he said, leaning against her doorway.

She smiled. "Hi. I'm OK. See?" She raised her arm, as she'd already done for Benji, Carol, and Aunt T.

"I'm so glad!" Brian sighed and sat down.

"Um, Brian, listen… I know we haven't even gone out yet, but things seem to be working out with my friend. So I'm very sorry, but I can't go on that date." Brooke flushed pink. "You're great. And if it was a different time, I'd be interested in more off-the-clock time with you. I hope there are no hard feelings."

"None at all. I get it, Brooke. I hope you two are happy." While his words were kind, there was sadness nestled in his eyes, and that broke Brooke's heart a little.

"Friends?"

"Yes. Friends. Of course." Brian said goodbye and walked out of her office. Brooke hated doing that. *He really is a nice guy.*

At that moment, her office phone rang, and she snatched it up, relieved to have something else to think about. "Detective Hill."

"The gun is a match, but the partial fingerprint on the camera was not a match for Don." Beal got straight to the point, seemingly similarly high on adrenaline—or, more likely, caffeine. His voice was an octave higher than normal, and his words moved at warp speed. She assumed he probably hadn't gotten much sleep, either, with all the activity related to the Reeses' case and the paperwork he likely did after booking Don.

"Shoot, about the print. That's weird—was it a match to anyone in the system?" she asked.

"Yes, and you're not going to believe it!" Beal.

"Who?"

"Officer Patrick Palasco."

CHAPTER 27

alasco? That's right! Where is he? Brooke remembered they had agreed to meet at the station, "first thing in the morning." She suddenly wished she'd put a time on that invitation as she glanced at the clock on the wall: *10:22.*

After hanging up with Dan Beal, she called the West Springfield division and left a message for Officer Palasco. "Tell him to call me immediately," she said. Her next step was to meet with Don Reese to see if he'd spill the reason Patrick Palasco's prints were on the camera that no one else knew about. *But I know that narcissist won't tell me anything unless I give him something in return,* she thought with frustration.

At 11:10 A.M., Brandon Evans walked into Brooke's office. He wasn't nearly as dressed up as the night before, now wearing a pair of tan slacks and a short-sleeved button-down plaid shirt.

"What, no suit?" Brooke poked fun at Evans, trying to build rapport. She didn't know Brandon all that well, but she assumed they'd be working together often in the years to come.

"I was still in my church clothes last evening, ma'am."

She stared at him. "I was kidding, Evans. It's OK; I don't care what you wear."

He gave her a lop-sided smile and continued, "I started working on the Reese case. Ann authorized me as a user on her alarm account."

"Great. And thank you—I assume from that pile that you've already found something?"

"Oh, did I!" Evans sat down across from Brooke in one of her wobbly chairs. "Don Reese 'broke into' their alarm system—several times." He used air quotes, Brooke assumed, since Don was still part owner of the home and the system. "He first tried to divert all the cameras to his phone instead of to hers—I assume that breaks the protective order?" Brandon looked to Brooke.

"It sure does. And there's concrete proof of this?" Brooke wanted to know that Don couldn't weasel his way out with some technological loophole.

"Yes ma'am. And when that didn't work because the alarm technician had come to their house and fixed things, he wiped all four cameras she had installed outside. Then he disabled the Smart Gateway hub." He pulled out several papers and pointed to where Brooke could find the information.

"What am I looking at, Evans? What is a Smart Gateway hub?" Brooke asked, not having the technological savviness to decipher the various tables and lines of data.

"It's the hub for the security system; it's what connects the security system to the station and the fire department. If it's down, when the security system is triggered, it won't alert us to the emergency."

"So, basically, it makes the security system useless."

"Exactly."

"When did he do this?" she asked.

"All the dates are here." He pointed to a table on the second page. "The disabling of the Smart Gateway hub, negating any call to police and fire, was… two nights ago."

"And you have proof that Don was the one who did this? We can trace it back to him specifically?" Brandon nodded, and a sense of relief washed over her. "It all goes back to his cell phone's IP address. You'd think he'd try to cover that up, but he didn't—real egomaniac that one. It's like he didn't care if he got caught… here you go."

Evans pushed the stack of papers toward Brooke. "All this tracks him taking the cameras down, when the cameras went off, when the Smart Gateway went down, and the data log showing his cell phone number and its corresponding IP address as the origin point for all this activity."

Her gut had been right, and she had Don pinned down. She had the evidence, including the gun ballistics, to keep Ann safe for a long, long time. "Wow, thank you, Evans. I'm going to call Mrs. Reese and head down to the magistrate to press charges for computer trespassing."

Brandon pushed his round glasses up on his nose. "Oh, I'm not done. I just got off the phone with the security company and told them what I found. I was transferred to the head legal person, who asked for copies of the evidence; they're looking at pressing charges against him too." He leaned back and smirked at Brooke. "I'm checking with our legal team first, of course. And… the camera you found?"

"I know; it didn't have his prints," Brooke answered.

"Well, I *can* tell you it came from his company—it's one of his company's prototypes. No one else makes something like that yet." His wide grin showed his perfectly straight teeth. "But it wasn't hooked up to the system yet."

"Sucks to be Don Reese right now." Brooke couldn't help it; a big smile covered her face, which matched Evans's grin. The two of them looked like they'd just heard the funniest joke ever told.

Brandon motioned to the stack of paper now in front of Brook. "Those are your copies. I'll email the summary report to you as well."

"Thank you. Oh! And do you have any updates on those Facebook messages Ann believes came from Don? Is there any way to trace them and prove it?"

"That's tough. I haven't dug deep into that issue yet—been busy with the other stuff. Basically, anyone can create an account or spoof someone else's to make it look like it came from them. I'll contact Facebook to see what I can find out—maybe get the IP address of the person who set it up. I'll need a warrant, though."

"I'll get one for you when I go to the magistrate with the new charges."

"Great—then I'll wait to look into it." Brandon stood up, shook Brooke's hand, and said, "It's been a good morning. Glad I could help."

"I'm sure we'll be seeing more of each other, Brandon. DV cases pop up all too often, and a tech pro is usually someone we need. Thanks again for your expertise."

————

After Brandon left her office, Brooke checked her office messages to see if Officer Palasco had called back. Negative. *Where is he?* she thought, with increasing concern. Before pursuing him further, Brooke called Ann. Maybe she could weave a few questions into their conversation that would help bring light to this mystery regarding Ann's *friend* Pat.

"Hi, Brooke." Ann sounded better than last night. Her voice seemed airy, almost happy.

"Ann, how are you?" Brooke took a sip of lukewarm coffee and cringed. Her stomach rumbled its discontent, and Brooke knew food needed to come soon.

"The kids and I stayed at our next-door neighbors' last night. We are at our house right now—but just to pack. I decided to take them out of school for a few days to go to Great Wolf Lodge. Do you think that's OK? Am I going to be needed for anything?" Brooke could hear Ann rustling around, probably stuffing items into suitcases.

"I think that's a great idea. I have some additional information for you." She told Ann what she'd learned about the alarm system. She left out the part about Don's fingerprints not being on the mailbox camera and whose were, as she needed to investigate that further. It seemed Ann and Officer Palasco were quite chummy, if not a full-fledged couple—she could half-understand why Don was so angry about them.

"I knew something was wrong, but I can't believe he did all of that! Of course, I can't believe he shot you, either. How are you feeling? And what happens now?" Her questions tumbled like laundry in the dryer.

"I'm fine, thank you for asking. He's lost control, Ann. That's what happens when guys like him feel their world slipping away. When I get off the phone with you, I am going down to the magistrate and will press charges for computer trespassing. I'm also going to find a judge to get a warrant to look into the Facebook account that's been harassing you. We're just adding to Don's jail time now."

"I don't know if I should be happy or sad about all this," Ann said truthfully.

"I understand..." Brooke knew this was the opening she was waiting for. "Ann, what's your relationship with Officer Palasco?"

"Pat?" The rustling on the other end stopped. "He's a friend. I work with his mom—well, used to. Because of everything going on, I've taken a leave of absence. Pat's been so nice and helpful, especially during this scary time... why?"

Brooke hated questioning Ann, but it was necessary, *for her protection,* she reasoned. "Just trying to locate him for our meeting this morning. That's all." Brooke knew loose ends became messy ends, and the camera situation was a loose end. She vowed not to let any more mess find its way into Ann and her kids' lives. "I'll text you when I'm finished at the courthouse and let you know what's going on."

"Thank you, Brooke. It's comforting to know that you're in my corner in this."

As Brooke hung up the phone, she felt the pride of a job well done flowing through her veins.

CHAPTER 28

Monday afternoon, as Brooke entered the courthouse building to file the new charges with the magistrate's office and secure the warrant with a judge on the clock, Greg Levine walked out in another expertly-tailored suit. As he held the door for a younger man in front of Brooke, he wore a smug look that matched his expensive clothes. But when Greg saw Brooke, he gave her a friendly nod and erased the wicked grin from his lips.

"Detective Hill, good to see you. Thanks for the heads-up last night," Greg said. Brooke was not sure if he was being sincere or sarcastic.

"Working on behalf of your client, I assume?"

"*Former* client. I'm no longer representing Mr. Reese."

"Oh, really? May I ask why?" Brooke didn't even try to hide her shock.

"Let's just say we had 'logistical differences.' I explicitly told him not to do what he *purportedly* did the last two nights, and he *possibly* chose to ignore my directives. I can't represent someone who is going to disregard professional advice and *presumably*, blatantly violate the law,… and shoot a detective. A public defender can take care of his legal needs at this point." His eyes betrayed the smallest hint of regret for his defense-attorney-biased lawyer-speak. Brooke had learned DAs will forever leave the judicial door open for any defendant's innocence.

Greg blinked, and his gaze returned to having an arrogant glint again. "Anyway, I'm sure I will be seeing you soon. Take care, Detective." He turned and walked down the steps to a waiting black SUV idling by the curb.

Well, this is unexpected, Brooke thought. She shrugged and walked into the courthouse to find an available magistrate or judge, her heels clicking on the marble flooring.

She didn't find Judge Southers, but a different judge, one whom Brooke had never before appeared: Emmett West. The middle-aged judicial sentry was dark-haired and sported wrinkles near his eyes and at the corners of his mouth. His dark, wood-paneled office smelled like oranges, and Brooke spied the offending peel in the wastebasket next to his desk. He didn't offer her a seat, so she remained standing in front of him.

As Brooke explained a bit of the backstory and the most recent pending criminal charges, he stared at the side wall, leaning back in his chair, with his fingers steepled on his chin. It made her feel awkward, but she forged on with feigned confidence, and requested the warrant to look into the Facebook account.

When she finished her appeal, Judge West sat mutely for several long seconds. Brooke glanced at the wall to see what had stolen his attention. There was a framed illustration of a courtroom scene, shaded with colored pencils. The artwork was mediocre, at best.

"My daughter drew that," he offered as an explanation. Brooke wasn't sure how to respond, and she felt sweat trickle down from her left armpit, where her bandages made her feel warmer than usual. "Hand over the paperwork. I'll sign the warrants."

Brooke pulled them from her bag and lay them in front of him. *Phew!*

The process of filing the new criminal charges with the magistrate went smoothly, too. Don would be back in the courtroom for the computer trespassing within twenty-four hours. She hoped it was enough to keep him behind bars.

Once outside, Brooke typed a message to Ann, alerting her to the favorable outcome with the warrant and criminal charges. Her next stop was to meet with Don, but first she called Beal to ask if he would accompany her. He replied instantly: "Be right there."

Beal was turning out to be a fabulous partner.

CHAPTER 29

As Brooke made her way to the interview room to meet up with Beal, then Don, she thought of Patrick Palasco again. *Is he the angel Ann thinks he is? Or is he a co-conspirator with Don?* Brooke shook her head, sure that there must be a logical explanation for everything. *That's ridiculous; of course he's not.*

Beal and Brooke sat down at the metal table in the nondescript, white-walled room and waited. A few minutes later, Don Reese and his newly-appointed public defender entered and sat in the two chairs opposite them. She was a young attorney with ginger hair, and who looked more like a librarian than an attorney, Brooke thought. Her long skirt and collared blouse reminded Brooke of Amish Country. The woman introduced herself as Sloan Bennett.

Before they began, Sloan advised her client that he didn't have to answer anything he didn't want to answer. Brooke rolled her eyes, then stared at Don, whom she noticed had dark bags under his eyes. They showed no less condescension than before, however.

"To what do I owe this pleasure?" Don asked with a heaping portion of spite.

"Tell us about your camera on your mailbox, Mr. Reese. We know it came from your company—some kind of prototype. When did you put it there, and why?"

"Mr. Reese, I advise you not to answer this question."

Don ignored his lawyer. "I don't know about any camera on the mailbox." His tone shifted ever so slightly, almost as if he was surprised by the revelation. His eyes flashed, but Brooke didn't buy it. *This guy is such a compulsive liar.*

"Really? Because I don't know who else would have put one of *your* company's brand-new cameras on *your* family's mailbox. Do you?"

"Nope. Maybe Ann?" He smirked as he mentioned his wife's name.

Beal jumped in. "What happens when we match your fingerprints?" Brooke knew Beal was utilizing a well-known interview tactic: pretending not to have as much information as they did in order to make the person on the other side of the table feel nervous and slip up.

"Mr. Reese..." Sloan Bennett's frown was as big as Don's ego.

"You won't. And if you do, it's because, as you said, it's one of my cameras—I could have touched it at work, and then someone could have stolen it." Don smiled, and his attorney fidgeted in her seat.

"Mr. Reese, just answer the question asked," she said. "Don't provide more information than what they want, please."

Brooke chuckled. This lawyer was out of her league and couldn't control her client. "Mr. Reese, do you know Officer Patrick Palasco?"

"Only as the dimwit who is sleeping with my wife!" he roared. "Why?"

"Did you know him before he started checking in on Ann?" Brooke was careful with her words. She didn't want to set Don off if there was no connection between him and Patrick; and she didn't want to give his new attorney any information to use in his defense against the charges.

"No. And again, why?"

Brooke smiled as an answer. Then she stood up and nodded to the guard waiting outside, whom she could see through the small square window in the door. "Thanks for your time, Mr. Reese."

"That's it? You're gonna make me go back to the cell? This wasn't nearly as much fun as I thought it'd be."

Brooke ignored him. But she grinned when his attorney shushed him. Beal stood and followed her outside to the parking lot where they could talk in private.

As soon as they reached the parking lot, Brooke turned to face Beal. "Before we get to Don and his reaction to the camera, let's talk about Officer Palasco. It seems he is avoiding me."

"He never showed this morning?"

"No. And I've left him a message, but there's been no call back."

"Interesting. First his prints, and now he's MIA?" Beal's face screwed up with the possibility they were dealing with a rogue cop.

"Seems so. I'm going to take a field trip over to his station, and if he's not there, I might talk to his supervisor. Care to join me?"

"Of course."

"We can talk about our strategy on the way there. Come on—you can hop in my car. I'll drop you back here afterward." She pointed to the space in the lot where her Camry sat. Beal nodded, and the two strode toward Brooke's car.

Once they were inside and buckled up, and Brooke was driving toward the West Springfield PD, Brooke broached the subject of Beal's career.

"So, Dan… we were at the academy together, right? You've known about my end goal since then, especially since being the head of a DV unit relates to my personal story. So I'm curious: where are you heading with your career?"

Beal chuckled. "Are you saying I'm lagging?" He knew Brooke well enough to know that was not what she was saying.

"Of course not; I'm sorry. I just want to know where you see yourself down the road. You're really good with these DV cases, especially with the victims—you strike the right tone, you're compassionate, easy-going... or maybe it's just the man-bun." She chuckled, too.

"Of course it's the man-bun." After a pause, Dan answered Brooke's question seriously: "I want to make detective too, I just don't want to go to homicide or the special victims' unit. I have kids now—girls—I don't want to go home after work and be reliving those kinds of horrors in my mind. Personally, I'm afraid the job would make my family suffer because I'd struggle with compartmentalizing and not knowing where the nightmares begin and end... you know?"

Brooke nodded but said nothing. She understood more than he likely realized, but she had chosen to dive headfirst into her personal nightmare. That was the primary difference between the two of them—that and that she was single, sans kids.

But I have Nick now. Even as she had that thought, Brooke knew it was different—her personal story came from her past and with Nick being an officer, they both understood the dark underbelly of humanity and saw the world through the same lens. Beal's wife and kids lived in a well-protected bubble of bliss—on purpose, no doubt.

"I'm sorry, that may have come out disrespectful toward your choices. I didn't mean it that way." He looked out the passenger window.

"No offense taken; I get it. Family is your priority, and it should be. So what about a police detective, say, in DV? I see there were a couple of openings posted last week under our LT. I could use a partner..." Brooke turned to face Dan in time to see a smile inch its way across his face. "I know there are nightmares—trust me—but it's rewarding work."

Beal sat silently for a few long seconds. Finally, he voiced his musings: "I was thinking the same thing over the last few days. Maybe it's time to make that move."

"Yes, it is. Go talk to Lieutenant Adams. And know I'll have your back every step of the way."

The two rode in silence. They were only a few minutes from the West Springfield station when Brooke's phone buzzed with a call—it was Dispatch. Her Bluetooth connected.

"Detective Hill. Here with Officer Beal." She didn't want any private or classified information shared accidentally.

"Detective Hill, I have Officer Patrick Palasco from West Springfield holding on the line for you." Beal gave Brooke a sideways glance, an eyebrow arched.

"Well, I'll be darned. OK, put him through," Brooke said as she pulled into the police lot. "He has emerged from the dark."

CHAPTER 30

"Detective Hill…" Officer Palasco's voice sounded muffled as it wafted through the car.

"Hey, Palasco, where have you been? You missed our meeting this morning, and I've been trying to track you down. Everything OK?" Brooke opted for a direct approach, but she laced it with kindness and respect. Palasco was a fellow officer, and he'd treated Ann with nothing but care and compassion, helping her and the kids through the worst nightmare imaginable.

"Yeah, sorry about that. Had an emergency with my mother, but she's fine now. I'm happy to meet with you anytime." Brooke let out a sigh of relief—he wasn't purposely avoiding her.

"What about now?" Brooke looked at Beal, who nodded. They paused for Patrick's reply, waiting longer than they'd expected they'd have to. "Patrick? Everything OK?"

"Um, yeah. Now is fine. Just getting my mom situated, but I can meet you. Tell me where." Brooke's gut was pinging with discontent, but she wasn't sure why.

After a beat, she answered the officer. "The station. *Your* station."

"West Springfield? OK… I'll be there in fifteen." The line went dead.

"He is a good guy, Brooke," Beal said, using Brooke's first name. She thought it might be to help reel herself in from considering the

163

obvious conspiracy theory. "He was behind us at the academy, and I knew him casually. Let's give him the benefit of the doubt, OK?"

"You getting soft, Dan?" She winked at him. "I'm kidding. And I agree with you—I'd just like to know the full nature of his relationship with Ann. Plus, he has a lot to explain with those fingerprints. Can't ignore evidence, no matter how nice a guy is… or if he wears our uniform."

She paused but then added, "But, of course, we'll tread lightly."

Beal nodded. They stepped out of the Camry and strode toward the doors of West Springfield, wanting to get set up in an interview room before Patrick arrived. Brooke had chosen his home turf as a way to make Patrick more comfortable—a classic move. But as they entered the building, she reminded herself to be curious, not judgmental. *Don't make any assumptions.* Officer Palasco had helped Ann in her time of need, and he was a fellow officer. *A good one.*

But Brooke knew she had to follow the evidence, too.

———————

As Brooke and Dan sat in the plastic chairs and waited for Officer Palasco in the drab, gray-painted room with a video camera perched in the upper corner near the ceiling, Brooke's phone buzzed with an incoming text. She pulled it from her pocket and took a peek. As she did so, she saw it was nearing five o'clock.

Meeting at your place tonight, right? For our talk?

Brooke smiled. *Nick.* She typed a quick reply: *Yes. I'll be there after 7… after all, it's my house.* ☺

She hit send. As soon as she did, she felt the sensation of her stomach dropping, as if she was flying down a rollercoaster's steepest part. Nick's text had been straight and to the point – no banter, no flirting. Maybe his objectives for "the talk" were different from hers. Maybe this was not something to look forward to but something to dread. Her heart fluttered with anxiety. *Not now*, she chastised herself. *Do your job. Worry about it later.*

Beal fidgeted beside her. Part of his man-bun had come undone, and a stray piece of blond hair was hanging behind his ear. She was just about to tell him about it when the door flung open.

Officer Patrick Palasco walked in, smiling and dressed in his uniform, complete with handcuffs, gun, and the various other weapons an officer has at his disposal. His piercing eyes caught hers, and his grin widened. Brooke hoped she was staring at a caring officer—an innocent man—but her eyes had spied the gun first, and her heart rate rose.

Back at the Courthouse, Don and his new attorney, Ms. Bennett, appeared before another magistrate at a new hearing for the additional charges.

The magistrate banged his gavel with his decision, removing any opportunity for bail—the charges against Don had been piled too high. His trial date was schedule for three months down the road. Even without the computer trespassing, this particular magistrate, a thirty-year veteran with silver hair, a crooked nose, and a bias toward the prosecution table, wouldn't have permitted any bond for this defendant. Any time you fire a weapon, you become a danger to the community, the magistrate believed, especially when your target is an officer of the law. He didn't care who you were or what standing you had in the community.

Don's shoulders slumped in defeat as the court officer escorted him to the waiting van that would take him back to his jail cell. What Don didn't know yet was that Mr. Evans, the IT guru armed with the new warrant from Detective Hill, had contacted the "powers at be" at Facebook. Mr. Evans had just finished digitally connecting Don to the new account that had been harassing Ann, adding the final pair of dirty socks to the top of the laundry list of criminal charges awaiting Don at trial.

CHAPTER 31

D espite the presence of the gun, Brooke dove into the interview, starting with forced pleasantries and creeping toward the condemning evidence of the fingerprints. She motioned to the camera above to alert the owners of the eyes on the other side of the wall to start the recording. The red light blinked on.

"Officer Palasco, we'll be recording this conversation. Is that OK?" she asked.

"Of course. But now I'm nervous—is something going on?" Patrick asked. "I thought we were going over the events at the Reeses' residence last night. What I saw and whatnot." His face showed no concern or worry; his voice was steady. He clasped his hands across his stomach and leaned back into the chair.

"Yes, we are." Brooke gave him a small smile. For the recording, she said, "This is Detective Brooke Hill and Officer Dan Beal with the Fairfax County Police Department, talking with Officer Patrick Palasco, with the West Springfield Division, to get his account of the events of the evening of June 21, 2023, at the Reese residence." Brooke stated the exact address for the benefit of the recording, then continued with, "First, Officer Palasco, can you tell me about the nature of your relationship with Ann Reese?"

"This feels awfully formal."

Brooke didn't move, didn't even twitch. "You seem to be over there a lot," she finally said.

The officer smirked. "We're not intimate, if that's what you're getting at. At least, not physically. I care a great deal for her and her kids. We're friends."

"Where did you meet?"

"My mom introduced us. She works with Ann." He stopped talking, and Brooke assumed from this point forward, he was only going to answer what was asked. He knew the dance; he had done it with others when the roles were reversed, she assumed, though he wasn't a trained investigator. He was a street cop. So... advantage, Brooke.

"When did you meet?" Brooke pressed.

"A year or so ago." He remained unfazed.

Maybe there is nothing he's hiding here. Let's try a different angle. "Had you ever stopped by the Reese house before the domestic disturbances escalated and the police were involved? So, say, a month or more ago?"

"No."

"Did you know Don Reese before all this happened?"

"No."

"He said he didn't know you, either, but he's not too fond of you now." Brooke smiled. It was a way to break some of the tension that had been building. An effort to tread lightly.

Officer Palasco nodded and frowned. "I imagine not."

"Do you want your relationship with Ann Reese to be intimate?" Beal asked.

"Why is that relevant?" No one spoke or made a move for several seconds. Brooke found his response interesting, and she waited a full thirty seconds before she jumped into the evidence. When she opened her mouth, her stomach tightened, a reminder to go slowly, as she'd promised Beal they'd do.

"Officer Palas—"

"Please, call me Patrick."

Brooke blinked. "I'd prefer to keep this more formal, if you don't mind."

She received a slight shoulder shrug in return.

"Officer Palasco, we found a camera underneath the Reeses' mailbox, pointed toward their home. Any idea why your fingerprints would be found on it?" Beal produced an enlarged photo of the camera, one Brooke had taken that night before removing it.

With little hesitation, the officer answered. "Yes. I touched it… I noticed it underneath there a bit ago. I don't remember what day it was—maybe three, four days ago? I thought it was part of the new surveillance camera system Ann's brother and the security system technician had installed after Don had the protective order mandated against him."

There it is. The plausible explanation, thought Brooke. But no sense of relief flooded her.

Beal, who had been mostly quiet until now, spoke up. "We didn't find any other prints on it."

Officer Palasco's shoulders went up and down, which they'd been doing a lot during the interview. "I wanted to see if it was securely attached. I grabbed it pretty firmly. Must have smudged any others if they were on there. I didn't think about prints at the time… you don't think I had anything to do with Don's trespassing, do you? I didn't— don't. I was helping Ann, that's all. You can ask her."

"I did ask her, and I saw how you've been helping," Brooke answered. "OK. Let's talk about last night." She rolled her shoulders and shifted in her chair. It had been hours since her last pain medication dose. Since it was getting late in the day, she hoped this next line of questioning went quickly. "Can you tell me your version of the events? From when you heard Don was in the front yard until the police showed up?"

"Sure." Officer Palasco blew air from his mouth before sharing his recollection of the evening. "We had finished dinner and were cleaning up. I heard Ann scream, yelling about how Don was back. I rushed to get the kids upstairs, something I think she asked me to do—I can't recall her exact words. But Ann met us at the stairs, and I guided Connor and Emma toward her, and she took them upstairs to hide."

"What did you do then?" Beal asked.

"I was planning to sneak out the back door, grab my gun and handcuffs from my car, which was parked in the driveway, and arrest Don. I was off duty and didn't want to bring those things inside, even though Don was still on the run. I never imagined he'd come back so soon... as I closed the back door, I heard the sirens. I never made it to my car."

"So where did you go?" Brooke asked.

"I remained downstairs in case Don tried to make entry before they could take him into custody."

"Did you notify the police who you were, that you were off duty but in the house, and that you had a gun in your car?" Brooke asked.

"Eventually, yes—once the chaos calmed down and they had Don in handcuffs. I didn't want to add to the seriousness of the situation and distract them from him—Don."

"Did you see the neighbor, Mr. Murray, at all during the events?"

"No. Had no idea he was out there or had called the police himself until later."

With the mention of the spy-like character—Mr. Murray—a yellow flag flapped in Brooke's mind, but she couldn't figure out why. She looked toward Beal. "Anything else, Officer Beal?"

"No. I think that covers it for now," he answered.

"OK. Thank you for your time, Officer Palasco. Appreciate it."

"Thank you... and sorry to keep you waiting today."

Brooke nodded. "By the way, how is your mother?" Brooke asked as she motioned toward the camera, indicating the recording could stop in the other room.

"Much better. Had a fall. She's OK, though. Thanks for asking."

CHAPTER 32

When Brooke arrived home an hour and a half later, she fled to the shower to wash off everything—and everyone—she'd encountered throughout her long day. Her shoulder was throbbing, and as she got dressed in jeans and a lacy, sleeveless top, she popped a couple of Advil tablets into her mouth, swallowing them without water. Looking at her watch, she realized Nick would be there soon.

As if on cue, her doorbell rang.

When she opened her door, her breath caught. Nick stood on the porch holding a huge bouquet of flowers, comprised of everything from lilies to gerbera, her favorite. "Hey there! These are gorgeous! You know what the red gerberas mean, right?" Aunt T's neighbor had been a florist—she'd learned all kinds of things from that woman.

"I don't even know what a *gerbra* is," Nick laughed.

"Gerb-era, not gerbra! And a red one means 'fully immersed in love.'" Brooke took the bouquet and waived him inside as she strode to the kitchen to find a vase.

"Well, then I picked the right color."

Brooke stopped and turned to look at Nick. His smile entranced her, and she forgot about the vase.

"Time to talk?" she asked. She laid the flowers on the counter.

He nodded, and the two made their way to the couch. They sat face-to-face, and Brooke tucked her leg underneath her, grabbing a pillow for extra comfort. She watched Nick run his fingers through his blond hair. His signature move always made her feel tingly inside, and tonight seemed to have an extra portion of tingle. She noticed he was wearing his police academy t-shirt, and her heart swelled with pride.

"I'd like to start," he offered.

"Sure. Go ahead."

"When the call came in that there was an officer down, and then I heard it was you…" Nick's voice caught in his throat, and he stopped.

Brooke leaned forward and rubbed his upper arm. "But I'm OK," she said, trying to soothe him.

"I know. And I know the jobs we have put us on the brink of danger every minute, and with any call or visit to a home or approach to a car, our lives are at risk… I know life is short. You getting shot opened my eyes. I guess you could say I grew up in an instant. And that's why I can't go on another day pretending…"

Brooke's chest tightened. *Oh, my gosh—he doesn't want to be with me? Is he saying it'd be too hard? That he was pretending to like me all these years?*

Nick continued, "I can't pretend that you mean less to me than everything. Brooke, for years, we've played this back-and-forth game. It's been fun and flirtatious, but it's been childish." He took her hand. "I have loved you from the first time I ever heard you say my name, and I've loved you ever since. The other women… they just filled my time. I can't go another minute without knowing we are together, as in a committed couple, who, I don't know, maybe someday is even more. I'm finished playing this game. I want to have you all to myself, and I want everyone to know it."

Brooke swiped away the tears rolling down her cheeks. "What about Liv?"

"I told you; I broke it off." His eyes peered into hers as if he was touching her soul. "What about you? That Commonwealth attorney, Brian?"

She shook her head. "I told him I wasn't available."

His eyes smiled before his mouth did. "I'm ready to commit, Brooke. I want to see if this works… wait, no—I want to *prove* to you it's going to work. I've never felt this way about anyone, and I'm finished running." Nick kissed her hand, then leaned toward her and kissed her lightly on the lips. "What do you say?"

The room was spinning, but Brooke didn't want the moment to end.

"Yes." It was all she could muster.

After they kissed again, harder and deeper, Brooke said, "This is either going to be the best decision we ever made or—"

He interrupted her by sliding his hands on either side of her face and kissing her again. "Don't finish that sentence," he said. "Let's just go with the first part."

———

That night, while Brooke listened to Nick snoring softly next to her in bed, she reached for her phone and started a group text with Cassie and Jacs.

Nick and I finally had "the talk." We're together. Like finally truly together. This might be it, guys. I'm so happy!!!!! GN!*

After Brooke signed off, she made sure her phone was on silent mode in case either one of them called or texted her back. Then she checked that her alarm was set for 5:30 A.M. *Tomorrow is only Tuesday?* She'd be in her new job for a week, and what a week it had been.

She rolled to her side, draped her good arm across Nick's chest, and promptly fell asleep.

CHAPTER 33

*F*eet pounding on pavement. Gun shots. Blood. So much blood.
Two cars speeding away. Blue and white flashing lights becoming smaller and smaller. Fading... gone!
Two officers dressed in black. Their faces obscured.
"Officer down!" someone yells.
Two officers run across the yard.
Two officers race down the street. Further. Further. Until they're gone, too.
Alone.

Brooke's eyes snapped open. Her lips felt numb, and her body was paralyzed. She lay there, unable to move or speak, but her heart rate was slowing with each passing second. Her eyes adjusted to the dark room. That's when she saw Nick beside her, sound asleep. *A dream!*

Finally, she could sit up. As she did, she reflexively reached toward her injured shoulder. Her mouth felt dry, and she longed for some water, but she wasn't ready to leave the security of her bed.

The echoes and images of the nightmare eventually scattered, leaving only one thought: *Where did the two patrol officers who were staked out at the Reeses' home go that night Don came back?*

She shook Nick awake as she whispered his name. "Nick! Nick…"

"Hmmm," came his sleepy reply.

"Nick, wake up." Nick's eyes opened, and Brooke swiveled to flip her bedside lamp on.

"Hey now!" Nick grimaced and rubbed his eyes.

"Nick, why did the patrol officers I asked to sit on the Reeses' house leave? They were gone… they'd left right before Don got there. Why?" Her breath was coming in ragged stops and starts as her adrenaline kicked in for the second time in only a few minutes.

"I don't know, Brookie. It's time for sleep; we'll figure it out tomorrow. What time is it, anyway?" Nick rolled to his other side, facing away from the offending light of the lamp, and pulled the sheets over his head.

"It's 3:30 A.M. I'm heading to the office, OK?" She kissed him on the back of his bare shoulder as he mumbled something indecipherable.

Once Brooke was dressed, her contacts were in, and her dark hair was up and out of her face, she drove to work, arriving just after four-thirty in the morning. She turned on the cheap coffeemaker in the break room, then, as it percolated, she left to turn on the computer at her desk. Staring at the screen as the hard drive puttered through its own wake-up routine, Brooke searched her brain for the names of the officers who were supposed to be camped outside Ann's house all the way up until Beal showed up. Nothing came.

When she smelled the reward of turning on the coffeemaker, she went to the breakroom, carrying her favorite mug. It read, "Kick down the next door," a gift from Jacs for her birthday a year ago. *And that's what I'm about to do,* she thought.

After filling her mug and adding a not-so-healthy amount of creamer, she sat down again at her desk. She heard the quiet chatter of only a couple of other people throughout the precinct. She checked the time.: 4:30. June would be coming in soon—she still seemed to live on European time, despite moving to the States a dozen years ago. *She'll know who they were,* Brooke hoped.

Brooke's computer finally fully kicked on, and she tried to search for the information, not wanting to rush June the moment the woman arrived. But she couldn't locate the records. "Come on!" she hissed under her breath, then sat back and sipped her steaming caffeine.

At 4:40, she overheard Mrs. Mary Poppins-Rogers' voice. "Good morning," June cooed to one of the detectives working at the table centered in the big room outside Brooke's office. Brooke stood up, smoothed her pink blouse and black slacks, and made a beeline toward June, biting her lip the entire way.

"Miss June, good morning," Brooke began.

"Oh, Detective Hill! What a lovely surprise!" June had on a flowery dress and long-sleeved sweater. Even though the summer pre-dawn air was already warm outside, the inside of the station was always cold. As June flipped on the remaining overhead lights in the precinct, Brooke dove ahead with her request.

"June, I hate to bother you right when you get here, but can you tell me names of the two officers that were dispatched to sit on the Reeses' home three nights ago? I made a clear request not to remove them from their post. But they left before…" Brooke decided to spare June the rest of the details. Her excitement was making her words flow fast and furious.

"Of course, dear. Hold on." She smiled as she moved toward her computer. "Have you gotten any sleep?" she eyed Brooke. Brooke nodded.

June's long, polished fingernails clicked on the keyboard. "It was Officers Blankenship and Warren in one car… and Officers Carrolton and Smith in the other." June gave Brooke their work-issued contact information.

"Thanks, June. You're a lifesaver!" Brooke hurried back to her office.

She sat in her flimsy chair and thought about how to ask the officers the burning questions swarming her brain—she didn't want to tick anyone off, or blame anyone, either. *Not yet.* Finally, at 5:30 A.M., she considered it late enough in the morning to make the calls. She started with Officer Bradley Warren, a decorated officer she'd known for years. He was a cool cucumber, and she liked him. She punched the numbers into her office phone.

"Warren," the officer said when he picked up.

"Officer Warren, good morning. Hope I didn't wake you. It's Detective Brooke Hill." She waited for his reply.

"No problem, Detective Hill. I've been up. What can I do for you?" *That's what I like,* she thought. *Calm. Cucumbery.*

"Three nights ago, you were dispatched to sit on the Reeses' home at 1516 Sherwood in Harbor Meadows."

"The night after you were shot?" Warren clarified.

"Yes," she said with some frustration. "The night Don Reese returned, and we arrested him." She'd made her point. This wasn't about her but about him and his partner right now.

"Yes, that's correct." Officer's Warren's voice was softer. *Message received.*

"Why did you and Officer Blankenship leave your post?"

There was a pause. "Patrick Palasco, an officer from West Spring-field, was off duty and inside the Reeses' residence that night. He assured us he'd watch them—that he'd be there all night. Said we weren't needed. We told him, 'No can do,' since he doesn't work in our district and wasn't a direct part of what we were dispatched to do. Told him we weren't leaving without an order from our commanding officer."

"OK, that's good, but…" Brooke prodded the officer along when he stopped talking. "Why did you leave then?"

"Well, that's when he said we should go grab dinner, that he'd watch the family for the hour that might take us. Said he thought we must be hungry. We'd been on duty since six A.M. And honestly, the four of us were hungry."

"So both patrol cars, the four of you, left at *the same time* to grab a bite to eat? You didn't take turns?" Brooke asked incredulously. While her ire was directed in part toward the offending officer, it was mostly building against Officer Palasco. *Seems he's more involved in this than he's willing to admit.*

CHAPTER 34

Brooke texted Beal to meet her in her office when he was able, then she leaned back and ruminated on everything she knew about the Reese case and Patrick Palasco. As she waited for her early morning meeting with Lieutenant Adams, she jotted notes and brainstormed reasons that fit both the fingerprint evidence and Palasco's dismissing of the two patrol cars. Some were innocent; others were nefarious. Brooke wanted to be prepared to give her boss a full update, even with the evidence still streaming in. It just didn't look good for this officer from West Springfield... Ann's new friend.

This would be Brooke's first official one-on-one, in-person meeting with the lieutenant since she'd become head of the DV unit; most of the communication had been done via phone or internal email. The truth was, Brooke really hoped to close the case entirely by day's end.

These thoughts reminded Brooke that she hadn't heard from Ann in a while. She hoped the kids were having fun at Great Wolf Lodge.

———

Two hours later, Brooke was back at her desk. She thought the meeting with Lieutenant Adams went well, and Brooke had even jumped at the small opening in their conversation to bring up Dan Beal and the two detective positions in the crimes against persons division. "I could use a partner, Lieutenant," Brooke had confessed. "The DV load is growing, and it'd be nice if one of us could be in court for some of these cases." Her boss had only smiled, but Brooke had assessed it as a positive smile.

The part of the meeting that did *not* make Lieutenant Adams smile was the growing evidence and suspicion over one Officer Patrick Palasco of the West Springfield division.

"Do they have a corrupt cop?" Brooke's boss had asked.

"Maybe, ma'am." Brooke had tried not to bite her lip. "We'll know more later today. I'm going to ask Officer Beal and Brandon Evans over in IT to look into a few things while I dig around in Officer Palasco's background. I don't suppose I can get a copy of his personnel file?"

"Consider it done. I'll request it from human resources and have a courier bring it to you. But we need to tiptoe, Detective. This is a serious inquiry that can ruin an officer's career in an instant."

"Yes, ma'am. I hear you." Brooke had promised the lieutenant she'd tread lightly—again—before returning to her office.

It was nearing the lunch hour when Officer Beal shuffled into Brooke's office, man-bun made up to perfection but with sleepy eyes staring at her. "Good morning," he croaked.

"Long night?" Brooke asked.

"Not long enough," he replied. "What's up?"

"Have you talked to the LT yet?" Brooke smirked, knowing full well their conversation about him going after detective had happened less than twenty hours ago in her car.

"Why do you think I was up so late? I put my name in the hat, as they say. Got Lieutenant's green light and filled out the application into the wee hours of the morning. I have an interview scheduled in two weeks with the panel."

"Way to go, Dan!" Brooke stood up to shake his hand. "It will be you. I have faith."

With a look of embarrassment, Beal asked, "So, what's up?"

"OK, then." Brooke walked around him to shut her office door. His eyes narrowed. "Can you and Brandon Evans in IT take a peek at Don Reese's finances? I'm also going to try to secure a warrant that will allow us to gain access to Officer Palasco's fin—"

"What?" Beal interrupted. "What happened overnight?"

"I had a dream, Dan." Brooke chuckled at the look on his baby-like face. "Do you remember there were supposed to be two patrol cars sitting in front of the Reeses' home the night Don returned—the night we arrested him?"

Beal's eyes flashed with instant recognition, and he nodded as he asked, "Where'd they go?"

"Exactly. Turns out your friend, Officer Palasco, told them to hit the road, to go 'grab some dinner,' according to Officer Warren." Brooke used her fingers to make air quotes.

"Palasco's not my friend." The two smiled at one another. She was going to love working with her new partner. *Hopefully, he's my new partner. They better pick him.*

"So I need you and Brandon to look for a money trail. That's the only thing I can think of for why our boy in blue would forgo policy, procedure, and all those hours of police training… oh, and the law and human decency. He must be connected to Don in some way. I'll dig into their childhoods and other histories. See if they ever crossed paths." Brooke shook her head. "And Ann is going to fall apart if and when we do find that connection."

———

After a quick vending machine grab of a bag of Doritos and a Pepsi, the winning combination for any lunch on the fly, Brooke closed her office door and woke up her screen saver to engage in a few minutes of online research.

Then there was a knock on her door. "Come in!"

A skinny black man in a Scooby-Doo T-shirt, high-top Air Jordans, and what could only be described as pajama pants entered. He was carrying a thick, sealed white envelope with Brooke's name on the front.

"Delivery. You Detective Brooke Hill?"

Brooke stared at the man.

He chuckled, then said, "I get that a lot. Sometimes, the police department uses me when they need something done real quick… and they pay me well to get it here fast and under the radar. My name's Harry. I used to work in the crime lab, developing the film before the department moved to digital cameras. Now I do this." His grin revealed two rows of perfectly straight teeth, one tooth adorned in gold.

"Well, nice to meet you, Harry. And thanks." Brooke reached across the desk to accept the file. It was stamped "Confidential" and sealed with enough packing tape to wrap fifty Christmas gifts. She bet there was a tracker inside too. *Maybe Mr. Murray helped them with the technology.* She giggled at her humor.

"Sign here." Harry directed her to his iPad. She used her finger to scribble across the screen. "Have a nice day," he said as he slipped back into the hall and shut her door.

After an extensive review of the paperwork, Brooke's hands were still empty. There was nothing in Patrick's employee file but glowing reviews, two accommodations, and a clean psych evaluation from four years ago. *Something changed,* she thought.

CHAPTER 35

After spending another hour perusing Don's childhood and college years, Brooke found something interesting. Don had a brother who used to attend the University of North Carolina at Chapel Hill. Palasco had grown up in the Raleigh-Durham area before moving to Northern Virginia as a teenager with his family. *Maybe that's the connection?*

Brooke found the number and dialed Don's brother, who now lived in Richmond. When Kyle Reese answered the phone and Brooke identified herself, he promptly hung up. *I guess Don already mentioned my name to him.*

Before she had time to come up with Plan B, her cell phone rang, and Brooke answered it.

"Hill."

"Brooke. We got him." Beal's voice hit her ear and made her breath catch.

She gripped the arm of her chair with her free hand. "Tell me."

"Brandon and I are looking at Don's business finances—and hopefully we can serve Patrick with the warrant for his finances next. Don's business paid Palasco $8,000 in $4,000 increments over the last two months. It's labeled as "security" in the books. I'll bet we find the same deposits on Palasco's end, even if they're hidden in some secret account."

"Great job! Oh, wow… Ann is going to be crushed." Then Brooke remembered Patrick Palasco's mother. "Dan, gotta run for another call. I'll be in touch soon."

She looked up Palasco's mother's number and dialed from her office phone.

"Hello?"

"Mrs. Palasco, my name is Detective Brooke Hill. I work at Fairfax County PD. How are you?"

"Oh, hi. I'm fine. And please, call me Debbie. Is everything OK, Detective? Is Patrick all right?"

"He's fine. I was talking to him yesterday, and he mentioned your fall. How are you doing?"

"Oh, dear. You must have me confused with someone else, Detective. I haven't had a fall. I'm at work now, can I call you back later?"

"There's no need, Mrs. Palasco. Thanks for your time." Brooke hung up. Now she had Palasco dead to rights for lying about two things. *His life is about to unravel even more.*

Brooke rushed back to the Lieutenant's office to tell her about the new developments.

"Bring him in," Lieutenant Adams directed. "I'll call his supervisor and the chief."

Then chaos erupted. A call came in for every available officer and the Fairfax County Fire Department. The county jail facility was burning, and evacuations were underway. "Don Reese!" Brooke shouted.

She and the Lieutenant made a dash for their cars, and Brooke was grateful she'd parked near the door earlier that morning. The weather had turned, and the clouds were releasing their contents like a raging waterfall in the sky. A gusty wind whipped at her hair and drove the rain at an angle into her face. Her smartwatch alerted her to a severe thunderstorm warning, just as a bolt of lightning streaked in the distance. She jumped into her Camry, turned on the portable blue flashing lights in the front and back windows, and buckled up. Then she raced out of the lot, her clothes soaked through. Two cars followed, all of them heading in the same direction and each splashing through the growing number of puddles on the road.

When Brooke arrived at the scene, she couldn't believe what was happening. A fire truck, its's ladder extended toward the roof of the facility, was parked to the right. Several firefighters were spraying the building with a hose, and on the opposite side of the street were three SWAT vehicles. About two dozen officers from various agencies surrounded a group of inmates, guns ready, as they corralled them to safety. Some inmates—she assumed the ones more prone to flight or violence—sat handcuffed in the back of several police cars. Everyone was drenched.

Brooke smelled the acrid smoke in the air and saw a plume of black swirls rising toward the clouds. The wind was still whipping, making the firefighters' work harder and more dangerous. The rain was a welcome addition, though—with its intensity, the flames seemed to be staying contained, and she estimated they'd have the fire put out soon. Brooke threw on her police-issue raincoat and strode toward the group of inmates being held on the sidewalk. She spied Don Reese in the mix. *Good.*

Without warning, someone yelled, "Freeze, police!" and everyone instinctively ducked. In her periphery, she watched as a uniformed officer pointed his gun down the street. Brooke ran, hunched over, back toward her car and withdrew her weapon from her holster as she went.

When she turned her head toward the subject of interest, she saw Patrick Palasco, standing near a row of hedges. He was about a hundred yards south of her position, facing away from the pandemonium. He wore black jogging pants, trail shoes, and a rain jacket, but she could tell it was him. In his gloved right hand was a large plastic gas can. *You've got to be kidding me.*

As Palasco started to turn to face the officer with the gun, the officer shouted, "Don't move! You're surrounded. Put down the gas can!"

Brooke looked around, and sure enough, no less than ten officers had their weapons trained on Patrick Palasco. Just then, Beal arrived on foot and crouched next to Brooke. Brooke saw the recognition wash over his face. "That's Palasco!"

"Yup."

They watched as Patrick put down the gas can and put his hands back in the air.

"Get on your stomach!" the first officer yelled over the wind. Brooke made her way toward Palasco, her gun still drawn, as he kneeled in the wet grass and slowly moved to the prone position.

Several officers approached with her. One of the patrol cops got to Palasco first, grabbed his arms, twisting them behind his back. Then the officer handcuffed him and stood him up to face Brooke.

"You're under arrest, Patrick. For a whole slew of things." She turned to the first officer who'd originally spied him slinking away. "Meet Officer Patrick Palasco of the West Springfield Division. Go ahead and read him his rights. Then he's mine. We've been looking for him."

The officer nodded. He turned to Patrick and began, "You have the right to remain silent…"

Threat neutralized, thought Brooke as she walked back toward Beal and her car. As she did, Ann's face popped into her head. She dreaded their next conversation.

CHAPTER 36

For the second time in two days, Brooke sat across from Patrick Palasco and next to Beal in a small, sterile room. This time, Palasco didn't have his gun strapped to his waist, nor was he dressed in his navy police uniform. He wore khaki jail garb that washed out his face, and his smile from the first meeting with Brooke was gone. A case representative and an attorney sat on either side of him, and none of them wore smiles either. The interview had started several minutes ago, with verbal jockeying between the attorney and Brooke, and then Patrick had laid out his request.

"You know I can't make these decisions, Patrick. But I'll take the information to the DA, see what he says. But first you have to come all the way clean." Brooke leaned back in her chair.

Patrick nodded. "I know."

"Let's start with why you tried to burn down the jail. Then we'll work backward."

"I wanted to hurt Don the way he tried to hurt Ann. I wanted him to fear for his life, to be afraid he was going to burn to death. I knew they'd put out the fire before anyone was hurt, but I wanted him to get the message. That it was me... that I was done being his pawn."

"Why were you his pawn?" Beal asked Patrick.

Patrick took a deep breath. "His brother and my brother knew each other in North Carolina. When I went back for a visit one time, Don was visiting his brother, too. The four of us were hanging out. I got into a bit of trouble. I'd already been accepted into the police academy, about to start actually, and I knew what I'd done would get me kicked out. So when the police arrived at the house we were staying at, Don took the heat for it. I owed him."

"What did you do?" Brooke asked.

His voice became a whisper. "Hit and run. No one was injured. But I left the scene of an accident where I was at fault. Don told the police in Raleigh that he was driving my car—that he had borrowed it from me."

"Why would he do that?… Don wasn't your friend or brother."

"I honestly don't know. But I'm assuming he wanted a future police officer in his back pocket. And it worked—he moved to Virginia, and he never let me forget it." Patrick closed his eyes and shook his head.

"Okay," Brooke said, "so is that why you planted the camera? Because he had you in his pocket?"

"Yeah. I didn't think it was a big deal since I knew I'd be with Ann and the kids most of the time. I thought I could protect them while still making Don think I was on his side."

"So if *he* was blackmailing *you*, why'd he pay you $8,000 and call it 'security'?" Brooke pressed.

"You found that, huh? He knew the blackmail wasn't going to be enough if someone got hurt. I think he really wanted to harm Ann, maybe even kill her… and he didn't care about his kids, either. They were what he called, 'collateral damage.' He knew I could turn him in anonymously, and if he hurt them, that I'd have no problem arresting him myself."

"So why accept the cash?" Beal asked. "Why keep up the charade and implicate yourself?"

Patrick's attorney touched his arm in a show of caution. Patrick brushed his hand away, presumably wanting to come *all the way clean*, as Brooke had said.

"It's the same story we always hear: I needed the money. There is a debt I had to pay. It's paid off now… from what Don gave me."

Brooke eyed him. "Gambling?"

Patrick nodded, not seeming to care that she had guessed correctly on the first try.

"What if Ann and the kids had been hurt or killed, Patrick? What then?"

"I wasn't going to let that happen. I knew Don's every move because he thought I was all-in with his plan. He thought I was his partner, but instead, I wanted to know what he was going to do so I could make sure I was there to protect them when I needed to be."

"You weren't there when I was shot." Brooke stared at the broken officer, now stripped of his duties, his reputation, and his freedom.

Patrick sighed and looked down at his lap. "I know," he said softly. "I'm sorry."

"Was it worth it?" Brooke asked, surprising herself with the trace of compassion she heard in her voice.

"No. No, it wasn't."

———

Brooke texted Ann to see if they were home from Great Wolf Lodge. Ann gave her a thumbs-up emoji, so Brooke drove to Ann's house.

When she arrived and rang the doorbell, Ann appeared in an apron. She gestured for Brooke to enter. When Brooke stepped inside, she smelled the distinctive odor of burnt chocolate chip cookies. "Kids got a little forgetful with the oven timer," Ann explained. "What brings you by, Detective?"

The formality is appropriate, I guess. Brooke smiled and waved toward Ann's sofa. "Can we sit?" Ann nodded and led the way.

Once they were seated and facing each other, Brooke started. "I have good news, Ann. The case has been closed. You're safe, and it's over."

Ann's smile told Brooke all she needed to know about the level of relief this good news brought the woman. It'd been a long couple of weeks.

"But there's some bad news too." Brooke wished she could crawl under the rug in the family room, but she made herself continue. "Ann, Patrick Palasco was in on some of what Don was doing to you and the kids. Patrick was the one who put the camera on your mailbox. He accepted payments from Don to keep quiet about Don's plans to come after you... to harm you."

The room filled with silence. Only the humming of the refrigerator could be heard. Finally, Ann spoke. "What?"

"I'm sorry, Ann. Patrick wanted to protect you and the kids on some level, but he was playing both sides. He had gambling debt— and he knew Don from before he was a cop—and Don took advantage of all of it. That's all I can say right now."

Ann brought her hand to her mouth. Then a guttural moan escaped through her fingers. "I trusted him! I know his *mom*!" Ann's voice had become high-pitched.

"I know. You must feel so betrayed, I'm very sorry." Brooke then stopped talking and waited.

After a few minutes, Ann spoke again. She seemed to have found some inner strength from somewhere. "I'm moving. The kids and I are going to Pennsylvania, back to where I grew up. We need to start over, surrounded by my family, their cousins. It'll be good for all of us."

Brooke nodded and grasped Ann's hand. "I think that's a great idea."

"I'll come back alone when it's time for the trial," Ann said. "Connor and Emma need time and distance. They've been through a lot."

"Don't worry about the trial just yet. Go, do what you need to do." Brooke wanted Ann to take care of herself and the kids first.

"Thank you, Brooke," Ann said. "You were a bright light in all this mess. I don't know how I would have survived without you—literally. We owe you our lives."

The two women stood up, and Ann hugged her. After a few seconds, Brooke wrapped her arms around Ann too. In those few precious moments, Brooke couldn't help but think of her own mother. She hoped she was smiling down from heaven.

EPILOGUE

Two days later

Brooke could finally breathe a sigh of relief. While she was unable to bring closure to Ann the first, or even the second time around, she knew Don Reese and Patrick Palasco were going to get what they deserved now. They were both in custody, with trials pending, and solid evidence awaiting their juries. She was hoping this fact would not only let Ann's mind rest a little easier, but her own as well.

This case had been tough for Brooke, but as with all things, the difficult moments and seasons are the ones that draw out the fortitude that sharpens people like nothing else. This case would be the first of many that would pave the way, she believed, for a long, rewarding, and successful career. After this, what could she possibly be afraid to face head-on?

Brooke looked at the time and decided that, instead of heading back to the station, she was going to drive home. After a restless night's sleep and a busy Thursday, she wanted to grab a quick nap. She could work on paperwork and other administrative tasks from home later in the evening.

Brooke parked her car in her driveway and strode toward her front door. She could almost feel the silk pillow waiting for her in her cozy bed. As she turned the key in the lock, she heard voices inside. Instinctively, she grabbed for her gun. After swinging the door open, she yelled out, "Hello?"

"Come in here!"

Cassie?

The cool air of her house hit her in the face, along with the warm surprise of seeing Benji, Carol, Aunt T, Jacs, Cassie, and Nick—all standing in her living room. "Cassie! You're back? And what are ya'll doing in my house on a Thursday at five o'clock?" she asked.

Cassie beamed at her.

"We are here to celebrate you, my friend," Jacs said. Her smile was contagious, and Brooke's look of surprise morphed into a grin.

"You got the bad guy, Brooke! You did what we wished could have happened before. In a way, you got some redemption for our family." Aunt T was teary-eyed as she spoke.

"And with your first case!" Carol added. She was holding hands with Benji, who nodded his approval.

Cassie came over and put her arm around Brooke. She whispered in her ear, "Mom would be so proud. I'm so proud. This time, evil didn't win."

As the champagne cork popped and everyone grabbed a glass from Brooke's open cabinet, Nick made a toast. "To my girlfriend, the golden-girl Detective Brooke Hill—long may she reign!"

Brooke laughed at the absurdity of his words. She was no queen. *But I am right where I need to be.* Surrounded by her family and friends, and with Nick by her side, Brooke knew she could handle any case that came her way.

A half-hour later, Brooke's phone buzzed with a new message. Pulling it from her back pocket, she read the name of the sender, and the hairs on her arm stood tall.

Sergeant Willows? She unlocked her phone to read the text.

Well done, Detective Hill. Keep up the good work.

The words seemed to flash at her from the text bubble. She laughed, more from relief than anything else. Before she could put the phone back in her pocket and turn back to her family and friends, it rang.

"Aren't you popular?" Cassie exclaimed with a side-eye glance.

It was Lieutenant Adams. "Detective Hill, you've landed a new case. Meet me at 9141 Blueberry Hill Lane. And call Officer Beal. We'll need you both."

"Yes, ma'am." Brooke replied. She tapped the end button and looked at her guests.

No rest for the bluecoats…

ACKNOWLEDGMENTS

This book would have never seen the light of day if it weren't for my amazing editor and writing coach, Cortney Donelson. Thank you for making my words and ideas sound so much better than I could have ever imagined.

Thank you to everyone at Morgan James Publishing for taking care of my work as if it were their own words on paper. Words will never be able to express my gratitude to everyone who has made this possible.

Megan Zavala, thank you for being the first to look at my manuscript and giving me hope that it would one day see the light of day in the publishing world.

A special thanks to Bobby Kipper, former Virginia detective and current director at the National Center for the Prevention of Community Violence, for ensuring the police procedures in my story are at least plausible.

I would be remiss if I did not acknowledge those most important in my life: my family, both blood and chosen. Thank you. Thank you for your continued support on this writing journey of mine.

Grace, Jack, Parker, Braden, and Hazel—being your bonus mom has been one of the great honors I have ever received. Thank you for being you and being so accepting (especially when I need everyone to be quiet because I am doing an interview).

Ethan and Tessa—my constant inspirations. You two make me prouder and provide more inspiration than I can ever tell you both. I love you to the moon and back (and then some).

Joe, thank you for being my biggest fan, my constant cheerleader, and most importantly, my best friend. I could not ask for a better partner. You and me.

And to you, for picking this book up, reading it, and hopefully loving it as much as I loved writing it. Thank you.

ABOUT THE AUTHOR

A. E. Lee started her career in Pennsylvania politics, and while she had hoped it would be everything like her favorite TV show, *The West Wing*, she quickly learned it was not. With the long hours, low pay, and even lower respect, she decided it was time for a change and embarked on a second career in education. She is now a beloved sixth-grade teacher in Fairfax County, Virginia.

She resides there with her husband and their beautiful children, where she continues her passion for writing. You can learn more about her previous books, her outreach, and her other writing at www.authoraelee.com.

A free ebook edition is available with the purchase of this book.

To claim your free ebook edition:

1. Visit MorganJamesBOGO.com
2. Sign your name CLEARLY in the space
3. Complete the form and submit a photo of the entire copyright page
4. You or your friend can download the ebook to your preferred device

Print & Digital Together Forever.

Snap a photo

Free ebook

Read anywhere

Printed in the USA
CPSIA information can be obtained
at www.ICGtesting.com
JSHW020839220924
70259JS00003B/188